JEREMY AND THE AIR PIRATES

N. ASKEN

Also in the series:
JEREMY AND THE AUNTIES

JEREMY AND THE AIR PIRATES

by

Felicity Finn

Illustrations by

Sally J.K. Davies

SECOND STORY *Press*

CANADIAN CATALOGUING IN PUBLICATION

Finn, Felicity
Jeremy and the air pirates
ISBN 1-896764-02-9

I. Title

PS 8561.I553J44 1998   jC813'.54   C98-930517-1
PZ7.F4966Je 1998

*To Matthew, who worked on this with me in utero,
and to Karen Ages and Derrick Early who took baby duty
so I could finish these illustrations. — S.J.K.D.*

Copyright © 1998 Felicity Finn

Edited by Gena Gorrell

*Second Story Press gratefully acknowledges the assistance of the Ontario Arts
Council and the Canada Council for the Arts for our publishing program.
We acknowledge the financial support of the Government of Canada
through the Book Publishing Industry Development Program
for our publishing activities.*

Printed and bound in Canada

Published by
SECOND STORY PRESS
*720 Bathurst Street, Suite 301
Toronto Canada M5S 2R4*

For Brian
And for our boys,
Allen, Henry, and Jesse,
with love

CONTENTS

PROLOGUE

Jeremy had no idea what he was getting into when he helped his mother make three life-sized stuffed dolls dressed as elderly ladies. From the beginning there was something mysterious about the three stuffed aunties known as Mabel, Gladys, and Dotty, who sat on his living-room couch in front of the TV. Jeremy soon discovered their secret. The aunties could talk! Not only could they talk — they were able to talk him into all sorts of things he really shouldn't be doing. The aunties craved adventure. They were full of shocking ideas and daring plans. Before Jeremy knew it, he was mixed up in shady midnight escapades that led to his involvement with the infamous, criminal Banks Brothers.

But the biggest mystery of all had never been solved: where had the aunties come from? And where were they going? Jeremy never knew what would happen next ...

Chapter One

TELEVISION HEROES

I SHOULD HAVE KNOWN the aunties were up to something. They had been unusually quiet for two or three days, and hadn't tried to talk me into any crazy adventures in over a week. They were sitting on the living-room couch, as usual, since they couldn't get off it without my help. Mabel, the oldest auntie, was dressed in a neat navy-blue suit and a black hat with a veil. Gladys, in the middle, was wearing a pink and grey flowered dress that was bursting at the seams. She wore large pearl earrings and her stockings had holes in them. Dotty, the youngest and most stylish of the aunties, wore a green and white dress and a flowery straw hat.

"We do not see much of you any more these days, Jeremy," Mabel commented. "Now that you've got a *real* friend."

They meant Rick, my best friend, the only other person in the world who knew about the aunties' amazing ability to talk.

"Oh, we're not complaining," Dotty added. "Not at all. It's very normal, very healthy, to want to be with someone like yourself."

"Rick's leaving tomorrow for Calgary." I sighed, wondering what I would do for a whole week of summer vacation by myself.

"I suppose you think it's boring," Gladys said, "spending time with three older ladies for companions."

They paused, waiting for me to protest that I *wanted* to spend all my time with them. I had given this problem a bit of thought. Although I usually liked the aunties, I couldn't imagine them interfering in my entire life. It was depressing. How would I explain them to a girlfriend — if I ever had one — maybe in about twenty years? Would I have this secret to hide all my life?

The aunties began talking about me as if I weren't there.

"I suppose we're not much fun to be with — not enough action for a young fellow. He wouldn't even miss us if we were gone," Gladys said.

"He might think of us now and then, with fondness" — Dotty sniffed into her handkerchief. "We did have some exciting adventures together. But he'd soon forget us. One does forget over time."

"Perhaps he would remember our many little chats in this room," Mabel said. "Can we hope that some of our advice on manners and proper conduct will stay with him? Or do we mean nothing at all to the lad ...?"

"We'll never forget *you*, Jeremy!" Dotty said passionately. "Even if you do forget us."

I was about to ask how I could possibly forget them

when they were always sitting right there on the couch, but the doorbell rang. The aunties froze into silent stiffness. No one would ever have suspected that they were anything more than three life-sized dolls made out of stuffed nylon stockings.

I went to the door.

"Hi," Rick said as he came in. I wondered why he rang the bell at the front instead of walking in the back door as he usually did.

"Good afternoon, Richard," the aunties said politely. He put his finger to his lips in warning.

Behind him, just coming into the front hall, were two police constables. Behind them were two men carrying cameras.

"W-w-what's going on?" I asked. I quickly thought back over the last few days, wondering what I had done wrong. I was sure I hadn't done anything bad enough to get arrested for. The aunties had a way of getting me into trouble, but we hadn't been in any for quite a while.

"Constable Rodney Heaves," the tall red-haired policeman growled. "My partner, Constable Sheila Barflie, and I are here to present you with a reward for your part in the arrest of the three bank robbers some weeks ago." He passed me an envelope while the cameramen took pictures.

I couldn't believe it! It had been so long, we had given up on getting a reward. I tore open the envelope. Inside was a cheque for a thousand dollars! My mouth dropped open.

"Stand close together," one cameraman said, as he turned on his video camera. "Could we move into the living room, get a little more space?"

"No," I said quickly. "It's full of — it's kind of a mess right now. My mom would be embarrassed if anyone saw it."

"Okay," the reporter said, "we need a bit of information for the news tonight. Can you tell us, was there anyone else who helped you boys with the capture of the Banks Brothers?"

"No, no other *people*," Rick said truthfully.

"Can you give us a few details of how you caught the robbers?" The reporter took out a pen and notebook.

"Well, um," I said, "there were these three old guys going around robbing banks in the city, and um, they hid the money they stole, and we accidentally found it, and they tracked us down and broke into the house here one night to try to get their loot back, and that's when we captured them."

"Single-handedly?" the reporter asked.

"Quadruple-handedly," Rick said. "Then we called the cops, and these two came over and handcuffed the Banks Brothers and took them off to prison and that was the end of that."

Constable Barflie was craning her neck around the corner, trying to see into the living room. Rick was doing his best to block her view of the aunties, but she must have caught sight of them because she said, in a sarcastic tone,

"I see you're still playing with dolls. At your age!"

I pretended I hadn't heard.

"Stay out of trouble from now on, you two, if you know what's good for you," Constable Heaves warned as they all went out the door.

"Personally, my partner and I don't think you deserve a reward," Constable Barflie added.

Rick grinned. "We'll spend it wisely."

"Thanks a million!" I called after them. I knew exactly how I was going to spend my share.

We went into the living room.

"Did you hear that?" I asked the aunties. "A thousand bucks! For us!"

"Quadruple-handedly indeed," Mabel said. "You know very well it was decuple-handedly. There were ten hands involved in that capture, not four."

"Yes, but we couldn't tell *them* that," I said. "You don't want *your* picture on the news tonight, do you?"

"Certainly not," Mabel replied. "We merely want credit where credit is due. You would never have caught those dreadful Banks Brothers without our invaluable advice and direction."

Split between two boys and three aunties, the reward came to only two hundred dollars each. I biked to the bank and changed the cheque into twenty-dollar bills. Fifty of them. Ten each. All the way home I was afraid I'd be robbed. But of course the only robbers I knew personally were safely in jail.

"The Banks Brothers went directly to jail and *we* collected two hundred dollars!" Gladys shouted.

The aunties got me to store their share inside the couch cushions underneath them until they decided how to spend it. It seemed a bit unfair that Mabel, Gladys, and Dotty were each getting two hundred dollars too. What could three stuffed dolls possibly need money for? It wasn't as if they could go shopping. All they could do was sit on the couch, exactly where my mother and I had put them when we made them nearly two months ago. The only times they'd been out of the house were when I had taken them. And then they had got me into so much trouble with bank robbers and the police that I'd promised myself I would never take them out ever again.

Rick was still there when my mom got back from work. She made hot dogs for supper and we ate them in front of the TV so we could watch the news.

"Watch closely, Mom," I said. "There's some really big news tonight!"

We heard the usual music and announcement: "Here is the C-KIT evening news. All the news you need from the people you trust."

The part about us lasted less than thirty seconds. "Three notorious bank robbers are now behind bars," the announcer said, "thanks to the efforts of two young local boys. Today they received their reward. Edward, Harvey, and Mortimer Banks were arrested recently after a cross-Canada bank robbery spree that came to an end in this city." A picture of the Banks Brothers appeared on the screen. Eddy wore a brimmed hat and had his coat collar up around his ears, Mort looked small and frail with wispy white hair and a hearing aid, and Harvey had a scar across his scowling face. There was a two-second shot of me and Rick grinning stupidly. Our names were announced as Jeremiah and Rich. Rick and I were disappointed, but my mom was thrilled.

"You're heroes!" she cried. "Genuine home-grown heroes. And you deserve that reward. I'm so proud. How are you going to spend your five hundred?"

"It's only two hun —" I began to say, but Rick gave me a kick. How could we explain sharing our reward with stuffed dolls?

"I'm getting a dog," I said. "I've always wanted one, and now I've got enough to buy one, as well as a leash and collar and doghouse and food, and —"

"No way," my mother said. "No dogs."

"Aw, Mom, I *need* a dog. I'll take care of it, I promise."

"Huh!" she replied. "That's what you say. I know who'll end up taking care of it. You're not responsible enough to look after a dog."

"You're always saying I spend too much time here alone," I reminded her. "A dog will be good company. Come on, Mom, please?"

"No dogs," she said.

"You can borrow Solange whenever you want," Rick offered.

"Ergh," I mumbled. Poodles aren't real dogs. Especially those little ones. They're just silly, yappy bits of fur.

After the news my mom went outside and we were able to talk again.

"How did it feel, being on television?" Dotty asked in a breathless voice. "Did it hurt? Did it feel odd being squinched down small enough to fit on that screen? Was it frightening being in two places at once, here and there at the same time?"

Rick and I looked at each other and burst out laughing.

"What are you cackling about?" Gladys demanded. "Can't you answer a civil question?"

"It's only a picture!" I said. "It's not like *we* were on TV. They just took film and showed it like a mini-movie. No, it didn't hurt a bit!" We laughed some more.

"Laugh if you want to," Dotty said. "I can't help it if I don't understand how television works. It's a very strange and mysterious contraption."

"It strikes me that television is rather like a time machine," Mabel said. "When we watched you just now, it seemed to be afternoon on television, even though it is at the present time evening."

Rick nudged me and I laughed out loud. Mabel looked offended.

"And what do you want a dog for, anyway?" Gladys asked. "Noisy, hairy, smelly animals that would probably nip our ankles to shreds."

"We ought to vote on it," Dotty said. "All those against Jeremy getting a dog raise your hand." All three aunties raised a glove in the air.

"Sorry, dear boy," Mabel said. "You are outnumbered. We agree with your mother. No dog."

I was going to protest that a dog would be a great friend. A dog may not be able to talk, but it can run and jump and play ... In fact, a dog would be just the opposite of what the aunties were: all talk and no action.

"Shh! Quiet!" Gladys ordered. "Our favourite show is coming on. Silence, please."

I groaned. The aunties' favourite show was called "Real Men/Ideal Men." A female audience got to ask male contestants all sorts of personal questions, such as "Do outspoken women frighten you?" or "What is the most embarrassing experience you've ever had?" The contestants were supposed to answer truthfully. It used to be my favourite show too, but the aunties had ruined it for me. They sat there criticizing and poking fun until I began to hate watching it. Tonight's theme was Communication.

"What do they mean by that?" Dotty asked. "Do they mean talking?"

The game-show host bounded onto the stage, smiling and clapping as the audience applauded. "Welcome!" he cried, "to 'Real Men/Ideal Men'! Do women prefer a man who communicates verbally or — with lah-di-dah-di body language?" he asked. "How does your ideal man communicate? Is he good on the phone? Does he write love notes or romantic letters, send telegrams or fly messages of love from a rented plane? Are his conversations primitive grunts, *u-huh* and *uh-uh*, or intimate fireside tête-à-têtes in which all is revealed? Is a lack of open and honest communication causing problems in *your* life?"

"That guy could use a few lessons on communication himself," Gladys said. "Who's he talking to, anyway? He acts as if the whole world is hanging on his words. Arrogant dolt."

"His pronunciation is dreadful," Mabel said. "He slurs his words and can't even use the Queen's own English. He ought to take elocution lessons."

"He's talking *at* us, not *with* us," Dotty said. "That is not conversation. Does he think we can answer his questions? If we talk back, he can't hear us in there, can he? The sound only travels one way, doesn't it?"

Sometimes the aunties were so ignorant.

"This is boring," I said. "Let's see if there's a movie on instead." I reached for the remote control to flip through the channels, but Gladys grabbed it and stuffed it under her large bottom where I couldn't get it.

"Why don't we go to my place and watch a video?" Rick suggested.

"That's *it!*" I shouted.

"What's what?" Rick asked.

"I'll buy a video machine!" I said. "If Mom won't let me get a dog with my reward money, I'll get a VCR instead. Our house is the only one for miles around without one."

"And, pray tell me, what might a video machine be?" Mabel asked.

"It's a machine you hook up to the TV," I explained. "You can buy or rent movies, stick them in the machine, and watch them on TV. You can even make your own movies if you have the right kind of camera."

"No," Gladys said. "You're pulling our legs!"

"I am not." I was nowhere near their legs.

"Do you mean to say," Mabel asked, "that you yourself could photograph people and things and watch them on your own television set? Surely not."

"It's true," I said. "Rick's got a video camera. Lots of people have one."

"My, my," Mabel murmured. "Life is truly full of surprises."

"All those in favour of Jeremy buying a video machine, raise your hand," Dotty said.

All three of them immediately raised their hands.

I should have known they were up to something.

Chapter Two

REMOTE ENTERTAINMENT

"A VCR?" MY MOTHER asked. "I don't know, Jeremy. Couldn't you think of something more educational to spend your money on?"

"How about a dog?" I said. "I'd learn a lot from having a dog."

"No dog," Mom said. "I know how much trouble you and a dog could get yourselves into. I guess a VCR's okay. We both enjoy movies ... What harm can it do?"

❖

When I finally got my new VCR all hooked up, Rick and I went to the library and borrowed a few videos to take back to my place. I made some graham cracker and Cheez Whiz sandwiches and we sprawled on the carpet in front of the couch for an afternoon of comedy.

The aunties took the humour right out of it. It's hard to enjoy a movie when three stuffed old ladies are keeping up a running commentary behind you.

"So you mean to tell us, young man," Mabel said, tapping her cane on my shoulder, "that that little book-sized gadget you poked in that slot is now running the television?"

"Yes," I said. "Sort of."

"Most mystifying," she said. "I do not understand how the pictures get from one machine to the other."

"They're hooked up with wires," I said, turning up the volume.

"*I* don't understand how all those people and animals and houses can be squaaaashed down into a little box and then squeeeeezed through a wire into the television," Dotty said. "It *must* be magic."

"Take a hint," I said. "We're trying to watch this, okay?"

"I don't know why they bother getting this sort of drivel into the television at all," Gladys said. "It's very low-grade humour. The show's been on ten minutes now, and there has not been one truly good joke. A nice steamy romance, now that might be amusing."

"Do you *mind?*" I said loudly. "I just missed a great scene, thanks to you three."

"Just rewind it," Rick said. He picked up the remote control and pressed a button. We watched the actors move jerkily backwards through the scene in fast motion.

Behind us the aunties gasped, then began to giggle.

"Look!" Dotty cried. "Look, they're all going backwards!"

Mabel's lips twitched. She giggled faintly into her handkerchief.

Gladys laughed a big, deep belly laugh. "Bless my soul," she bellowed. "Now, *that's* what I call funny!"

The aunties laughed so hard that Dotty was bouncing with hiccups and Mabel was nearly choking. We rewound way past the scene we wanted, just to watch them. Gladys laughed so hard she actually fell off the couch and landed face down on the floor between us. She lay there jiggling, her stuffing shaking.

"I'm *trying* to stop," she chuckled. "Mercy! I've never seen anything — hoo haw — so ding dong doggone funny in my whole life! Hee hee hee. You'd better — har har — set me — hoo hoo — back on the couch before I burst my — burst my — burst my seams!"

By this time Rick and I were laughing so much we couldn't move either. It was quite a while before we calmed down enough to get Gladys back between Mabel and Dotty, and get the movie restarted. I didn't want to see the first ten minutes again, so I fast-forwarded to the scene we'd stopped at.

The aunties began laughing harder than ever. Dotty jabbed her cigarette holder at the screen and gasped in helpless delight. Mabel was dabbing at her eyes, although of course there were no tears. "I do believe I am having a conniption," she murmured weakly. Gladys was quaking with laughter and making loud snuffling noises into a cushion.

"All this over *fast forward*?" Rick asked.

"More, more! Do it again!" Gladys cried. "I missed half of it while I was snufflecating."

We ran the movie backwards and forwards a few times,

until the humour wore off, and then kept the aunties quiet by giving them the VCR manual to read. To my surprise they actually seemed to find it interesting. It kept them quiet for nearly fifteen minutes.

Then Gladys poked her umbrella into me.

"How about the TV manual too?" she said.

"Haven't got one."

"How do you know how the TV works, then?"

"You just turn the knob and it works."

"But *how* does it work?"

"I have no idea. Who cares?"

"We do."

"Well, I don't, and I'm watching a movie, so would you kindly keep your mouths shut?"

"Our mouths are never open," Gladys pointed out. It was true. The aunties' mouths were stitched onto their stuffed-stocking faces and filled in with lipstick. They could move a little, but not open.

"So how about going to the library and getting us some books about TV?" Gladys asked.

"I thought you hated TV."

"We have a low opinion of what's *on* TV," she replied. "But its inner workings, its guts, so to speak, are quite intriguing."

"I have a great idea," I said. "Rick, let's take this video over to your place, where we can watch it in peace and quiet."

"Before you go," Dotty said, "would you mind bringing us the diary?"

I fetched their favourite book, the diary of an old photographer who had taken the last picture of the aunties in their real life. My mother had found this picture, an old-fashioned tintype, in an antique shop, and it had given her the idea for making auntie dolls. The aunties spent hours studying the diary, as if they might somehow learn from it just how they had been suddenly transformed from live ladies in a photo studio into stuffed dolls on my couch.

"By the way, dear boy," Mabel asked, "do you happen to know the price of gold these days?"

I looked at her. "Do I look to you like someone who keeps that kind of information handy in my head?"

"No," Gladys said. "You look like the type who doesn't keep much in his head at all." She laughed her deep, loud laugh.

"Now, please don't forget our library books," Dotty added. "Anything at all about TV — and could you possibly look for some books about fashion in the twenties, as well?"

I shrugged. "If I get the time."

Rick and I went to his place to watch the video in peace. Without the aunties it didn't seem very funny. Maybe they were right: it *was* low-grade humour.

"You know what would be *really* funny?" I said.

"What?"

"If the aunties laughed at a movie like this run backwards," I said, "what would they think of a movie of *themselves* run backwards? They'd laugh themselves sick! You've got a video camera. All we need is an empty tape and we can make the funniest home video ever."

"I wonder if they *can* laugh any harder than they just did," Rick said. "They might actually laugh their heads off. That would be kind of horrible to watch." He hopped off his bed to look for a blank tape.

Rick had everything in his room: his own computer, printer, fax, TV, VCR, phone, answering machine, and dozens of videos and video games. His mother was rich and whenever she came to visit Rick she spoiled him rotten.

"The aunties have ruined so many shows for me with their comments that I'd just *love* to criticize a video of them, in front of them," I said.

"You don't think it might be a bit — risky?" Rick asked.

"What do you mean?"

"Well," he said, "what if we made a video of the aunties and it zapped them back to where they came from? That's how they got here, isn't it? Through the TV?"

"Well, I guess so," I said. "According to the photographer's diary, he was trying to project the first-ever TV pictures the day the aunties were at his studio."

"And look what happened," said Rick. "By accident he projected the aunties clear through space and time into your living room. I think we should be careful. Putting them on film and back into the TV could be dangerous. What if we — lost them?"

"I doubt very much if we could get rid of them that easily," I said. "Putting a video of them on TV isn't going to make them suddenly disappear." I began to think about the possibility, though. Would it ever be great if I *could* get rid of the aunties whenever I wanted, just by sticking a video in the machine. It would be a perfect threat to hold over their heads whenever they started bossing me around. "Quit trying to run my life, or I'll zap you in the machine!" I'd say, and they'd have to smarten up or I'd do it. Of course, I'd let them back out of the VCR when I thought they'd learned their lesson, and when I wanted their company. I'd only have to have them around when I wanted. It would be fantastic. Sure, I liked the aunties — most of the time — but sometimes I just wanted to do what I wanted, when I wanted, without three old ladies constantly interfering.

"I think it's worth the risk," I said. "If we zap them out of existence, well, that's a chance I'm willing to take."

Rick looked shocked. "How can you say that? I thought you *liked* the aunties! Wouldn't you miss them? I sure would."

"You don't have to live with them," I pointed out.

The phone rang. Rick picked it up.

"For you," he said.

"Me? Hello?"

"Hello, Jeremy. It's Dotty!" She giggled.

"What? What are you doing calling me?"

"The girls and I just wanted to say hello," she said sweetly. "And see how you're doing."

"Since when have the three of you taken to using the phone?" I shouted.

"Ages ago," she said. "We often call Rick."

"I know you've called *him*, but —"

"And Gladys just loves calling the Radio Noon Phone-In. She calls at least once a week. Yesterday she actually got on the airwaves, and got to give her opinion of the Premier of Ontario."

"What!"

I heard a muffled conversation in the background and then Gladys came on the line.

"Hello, Jeremy. This is Gladys. HELLO, CAN YOU HEAR ME?"

"Lower your voice!" I said. "What's all this about you three using the phone? You'd better not be making any long-distance calls!"

"Relax," Gladys said. "Haven't you heard of 1-800 numbers? They're free! We call all the toll-free numbers in magazines and on TV."

"What for?"

"For the pleasure of speaking with other adults, of course," she said. "Do you think we enjoy talking to nobody but boys day after day? It's a new way of *communi-cating!*"

"You'd better quit fooling around with the phone," I said, "before you get us all into trouble."

"Don't worry. We only do it when your mother is out. Or sleeping. Did you know that you can call Sears depart-ment store twenty-four hours a day?"

"You called Sears?"

"Just a minute," Gladys said. "Hold the phone. Mabel wants to talk to you too."

"Hello," said Mabel. "Is this Jeremy?"

"Of course it's me," I said.

"This is Mabel here, now speaking, on the other end of the line."

"I know that," I said.

"Modern technology is truly a remarkable thing," she said. "Do you not agree? Here I am at your house, and there you are at Rick's house, yet we can hear each other clearly. Is that not amazing?"

"Right," I said. "What century did you come from?"

"No need for sarcasm," Mabel said. "It is especially offensive on the telephone. Of course there were tele-phones in our day, but we used them for emergencies only."

"This is an emergency?" I asked.

"Yes," Mabel said. "We have a small technological problem."

"Hey, it better not involve my VCR!" I warned them.

"Don't you three go messing around with my stuff while I'm gone. Hands off!"

"It regards the telephone," Mabel said, "and I do hope you can find it possible to answer civilly when you are asked a polite question. I merely wish to know how to find the number of a certain business. We could find no Toronto numbers in the telephone directory."

"What do you want to call a business in Toronto for?" I asked. "I warn you, if you run up any long-distance charges on my mom's bill we're in major trouble."

"We would not dream of incurring household expenses while we are guests in someone's home," Mabel said coldly. "There is a free 1-800 number. Unfortunately, the magazine in which we saw the advertisement has been removed from the coffee table."

"Just what are you guys up to?"

"We are not 'guys,' nor are we 'up to' anything, my dear boy. We are adult women who wish to be as independent as we possibly can be, given our obvious physical challenges. Do you wish to help us or not?"

"Okay, okay," I said. "Dial 411. If you know the name, they'll give you the number."

"Thank you," Mabel said. "We appreciate your cooperation. Goodbye, dear boy."

I slammed down the phone.

Rick raised an eyebrow. "What was that all about?"

"I'd rather not think about it," I said. "I have the feeling

I just helped them do something I'll wish I hadn't. Something's got to be done about them. I can't go on living like this. Let's go video them. I doubt it will get rid of them, but at least they'll be able to see for themselves how bossy they really are. Maybe they'll learn something from seeing themselves the way I see them."

I had another idea. "Just a second." I picked up the phone and dialled my own number. It rang and rang.

"I just wondered," I said to Rick, "if the aunties would *answer* the phone. Thank goodness they don't go that far."

Just then a voice on the other end said, "Halloooo?"

"Is Jeremy there?" I asked.

"Wrrrong numberr. Sorreee." The phone was hung up with a loud click.

"I bet that was Gladys!" I said. "I bet they've been answering the phone for weeks. This is disgusting!"

I pressed redial.

After about ten rings, the same voice said, "Halloooo?"

"Look, Gladys," I said, "it's Jeremy. What's the big idea answering the phone? I could have been anybody!"

"So why did you call if you don't want us to talk to you?" she said in a smart-alecky voice. "Why did you call and ask for yourself when you know perfectly well you're not at home?"

"I phoned to see if the three of you were *answering* the phone too."

"Occasionally," she said. "Only when we're really

bored. We were going to watch one of the other videos you got from the library. But Mabel said you said we had to keep our hands off your machine. I told her I would only reach across and touch it with my *gloves*, but you know Mabel. She said that would be twisting your meaning for our own selfish purposes. That's why I answered the phone. I had nothing better to do."

"Oh, fine, go ahead and use the VCR," I said. "If you're sure you can do it without breaking it."

"Of course we can," Gladys said. "We watched you do it. If you can do it, we certainly can."

"I thought you thought TV was shallow and disgusting," I said.

"It is," Gladys replied. "These video movies are a different story, though. No commercials. Two whole hours without a single stupid interruption. It's wonderful. And not only that, but you can run them backwards and forwards with the remote control. It's hilarious!"

"Well, I'm glad you like comedy so much, because Rick and I have a big surprise for the three of you." I grinned at Rick.

"What — a new movie?" Gladys asked.

"Sort of." I put my hand over the receiver so she wouldn't hear me laugh. "You'll have to wait and see."

Chapter Three

COMMUNICATION BREAKDOWN

WHEN WE GOT BACK to my place, the aunties seemed pleased to see us.

"Gladys said you have a surprise for us," Dotty said eagerly.

Rick held up his camcorder. "Showtime," he said, pointing it at the aunties.

"Fire that weapon and I'll shout the house down," Gladys bellowed, raising her umbrella. "En garde, girls! Defences!"

Mabel brandished her cane and Dotty aimed her purse.

"Relax," I said. "It's only a camera."

"Oh," said Gladys. "For a minute I thought it was a machine-gun. So that's what cameras look like nowadays, eh?"

I had forgotten that the aunties had never seen a modern camera. "This little machine," I explained, "is a video camera. We'll take a movie of you, and in a few minutes we can stick it in the VCR and see it on TV. We can even run it backwards. It'll be a scream."

"Just act natural," Rick said. "Pretend I'm not here. Just talk and joke as usual. You don't even have to look at the camera."

The aunties glared at us.

"Maybe it would be better if I interviewed them," I said. "You know, get them started with a few questions, such as: 'If someone tried to run your life for you, what would you do about it?' Something like that."

"I forbid you, Richard, to turn on that machine," Mabel said in a very cold voice. "Put it down at once, and please do not mention using it again."

"What's the big deal?" I asked. "Don't you want to see yourselves on TV?"

"Certainly not!" Mabel said. "The television is the last place we wish to see ourselves. I can imagine nothing more horrifying!"

"Oh, Jeremy, surely you remember what happened the last time we had our picture taken," Dotty said with a catch in her voice. "Snapped out of our time and flashed through space into yours — you can't imagine!"

"You are a very thoughtless boy. Very inconsiderate of our feelings," Gladys said. "Some surprise," she added. "It's rude to barge in and aim that thing at people without even asking their permission. It's an invasion of privacy. We could probably sue you. Besides, how dare you attempt to put us in the idiot box? You know how we feel about that vulgar machine."

I did know, but that didn't stop the aunties from lecturing us for ten minutes on the stupidity, violence, cruelty, sarcasm, and weak plots on TV. Then they went on about the silly commercials and bad acting and phony program hosts and predictable shows that always ended happily right on the hour or half-hour.

"But the worst thing is those moronic laugh tracks," Gladys said. "Canned giggles and artificial crowd guffaws so the audience will know when something 'funny' has been said. I can't believe people actually like watching fake people living fake lives."

"That's what I do," I said. "Even when the TV is off."

The aunties looked puzzled.

"I mean I watch you," I said. "You're fake people leading fake lives."

There was a long silence.

"We beg to differ," Mabel said. "We may appear to be 'fake people,' as you put it, but we are anything but artificial. Although we are handicapped by the lack of movable bodies, our lives are as full and rich as we can possibly make them. More interesting, it seems to me, than your own."

"Our mental activity has become stronger to compensate for our physical inactivity," Dotty said.

"Ho," I said, "you do nothing but sit on the couch all day. You can't make a move without me. You can't do a thing unless I take you out."

"If you think we're dependent on you for everything, then ding dong, you're wrong," Gladys said. "We don't need you any more than you need us."

"Get stuffed," I said rudely.

"Get a life!" they said, even more rudely.

"Come on," Rick said. "Don't argue all the time."

"I suppose you forgot our library books," Gladys said. "And didn't we ask you a couple of days ago to find us some old maps of the city? Did you do that?"

"No, you didn't ask me, and anyway, what do you want with old maps?" I asked.

"We just want to see all the changes in the city since our day," Dotty said sweetly.

"If you think you can talk me into taking you on an outing, you're dreaming. Whenever I listen to you I get into trouble."

"Don't be a boring bully," Gladys said. "Just find us a map."

"And while you are out," Mabel said, "perhaps you would be good enough to stop at the bank and change our reward money into —"

"No, no, and no," I said. "I'm not your servant, and I'm on to your tricks. I know you're planning something, but this time you can count me out. I'm not taking you anywhere and I'm not helping you with anything."

"My!" said Dotty. "Ask a simple favour ..."

"We depend on his kindness, never complaining about our own limitations, and what do we get?" Mabel asked sadly. "Cruel disregard of our wish for harmless pleasure. Callous indifference and coarse brutality."

"I dare say it's puberty," Gladys said, shaking her head. "Remember that show on TV about boys his age? Their minds and emotions are unable to keep up with physical changes."

I could feel my face getting red and my jaw clenching up. I took a couple of deep breaths. I wasn't going to let them make me mad.

"Your mother left you a list of things to do, Jeremy." Dotty pointed to a note taped onto the TV where I'd be sure to see it. It said, "Take out the compost. Buy milk. Clean the toilet. Clean the garage."

"I think it would be best if we all set about our chores," Mabel said. "Jeremy, your mother wishes you to clean the lavatory."

"The what?"

"She means the loo," Gladys said. "The powder room. The can. The bog. The john. Get a move on."

"And what chores do you three have?" I asked.

"We must clean out our purses, mustn't we, girls?" Dotty said.

"See what they're like?" I said to Rick as we went out. "You can't win. They're always twisting things to make me feel bad. They're always right and I'm always wrong, no matter what I say. I'm sick of them, I really am."

"I think they're funny," Rick said.

Rick took the vegetable scraps out to the compost bin and went to the store for milk while I scrubbed the toilet. I decided to save the garage for a rainy day. We went back into the living room. Rick wanted to read the comics.

The aunties had emptied their purses. The contents were spread out all around them. They had large purses and it was surprising how much they held.

"We shall divide the contents into two piles," Mabel said. "Necessities and incriminating evidence. Then we shall review them."

"Incriminating evidence?" I asked. "What do you mean?"

"It is not necessary to concern yourself in our affairs," Mabel said. "We have a systematic method of cleaning our handbags, that is all."

"This is one project you really can't help us on," Gladys said, and nudged Dotty.

Their piles of stuff didn't look systematic to me. They sorted busily for several minutes.

"Now," said Mabel, indicating a small pile on her lap, "here are the few things I consider necessary. I have, after some thought, reluctantly discarded my newspaper articles on child-raising." She indicated a thick folder of clippings. Also my comb and brush, which are, unfortunately, made of plastic. Neither have I any use for this ring of old-fashioned keys, thoughtfully placed in my purse by Jeremy's mother to add an authentic touch. I have kept only the bare essentials: my glasses case, my spare hairnet and pins, a fountain pen and paper, pencils, my sewing kit, a small first-aid kit, and my change purse. Now, Dotty, you are next. What do you consider necessary?"

"My pocket mirror, my cigarette holder, and my fan, of course," Dotty said, dropping the items back into her purse as she named them. "A spare pair of gloves, these lovely tortoiseshell combs, my lavender talcum powder, two pairs of earrings I dearly love, my change purse, and this pack of Kleenex."

Mabel nodded. "Very good. Except for the Kleenex. Please replace it with your handkerchief."

"Must I?" Dotty asked "This Kleenex is so soft, and you never need to wash it ..."

"No Kleenex," Mabel said firmly. "Now, Gladys, are you finished?"

"Well," said Gladys, "you're asking the impossible. The very things I want in my purse are the ones you'll say I can't have."

"I must insist," Mabel said. "I am sure you will agree that this is a necessary and wise precaution."

"All right," Gladys said. "My wallet, which is empty at the moment, my knitting needles and balls of wool, a deck of Snap cards, my spare hairpin, this old but good pocket watch, my jack-knife, and this useful ball of string. Then there's my licorice, chewing gum, peppermints, red blazers, and jawbreakers. Now, don't object — just because we don't eat doesn't mean we shouldn't be prepared. I feel better having it in my purse. It's comfort food. And this little bottle of sherry. I've also got this Mickey Mouse flashlight with eight extra batteries, and —"

"Certainly not," Mabel said firmly.

"Hey, isn't that *my* flashlight?" I reached over and took it. "I've been looking for this."

"I need it more than you do," Gladys said.

"No," said Mabel, "it belongs to Jeremy."

Gladys made an ugly face at me, then went on with her list. "I've also got these handy ballpoint pens, an extra sweater, plastic bags of various sizes" — she pulled out three or four green garbage bags, some grocery bags and milk bags — "a bunch of elastic bands, my mouth organ, a couple of *Reader's Digests*, and this exciting crime novel I'm right in the middle of."

"Please be sensible, Gladys," Mabel said. "You know what is at stake. No flashlight, no plastic bags, no elastic bands or ballpoint pens — no modern contrivances of any sort. Which year was your crime novel published?"

Gladys looked inside the front cover. "Let's see — 1962."

"Then I am afraid it is far too modern for our purposes. The magazines as well."

Gladys looked sulky but placed them on her reject pile, which included a wad of Kleenex, several comics I'd been looking for, two overdue library books, a can of ginger ale, some antique postcards, a wrinkled stocking, a squirt gun, and an old photograph.

"Hey," I said, "how come you're throwing out this old photo of yourselves?" It was the original tintype photo of the three of them sitting on the sofa in the photo studio long ago.

Mabel looked flustered. "We are not getting rid of it, dear boy. Please leave it there on the coffee table. It is of the utmost value to us, being our only possession of days gone by."

"You three sound as if you're packing for a trip or something," I said. "I hope you don't think I'm taking you anywhere, because there's no way. I'm not taking you one step out of this house and that's final."

"Aw, sit on it," Gladys said. "Mind your own beeswax and we'll mind ours. Who asked you for anything?"

The other two ignored me. I glanced over at Rick for some support, but he was lost in a comic book.

"Now then," Mabel was saying, "we must all check our change purses carefully. We cannot risk carrying any coins upon our persons that are dated" — she lowered her voice — "before a certain year."

"Hey, Rick," I said. "Let's get out of the house and play some tennis."

"Oh, boys," Dotty said sweetly, as Rick closed his comic, "we have a small errand we'd like you to run for us, haven't we, Mabel?"

"What is it?" I asked suspiciously.

"Would you be so kind as to take our money out of the

couch cushions?" Mabel asked. "And exchange it at the bank for gold?"

"Gold?" I said. "Are you kidding? They wouldn't give gold to a couple of kids — if they even keep it at the bank. What do you three want with gold anyway?"

"Gold is a stable currency," Gladys informed us. "By that I mean that it's valued the world over, in any country, in any time period. It's much more useful than paper money."

"You only have six hundred bucks," Rick said. "Do you know how much gold that would buy you?"

"Three bars?" Dotty guessed. "Six?"

"An ounce and a bit," Rick said. He knew about these things, being rich.

"Is that really so?" Mabel asked.

Rick nodded. He unzipped the couch cushions and took out the aunties' money.

"What about gold jewellery?" Dotty asked. "What could six hundred dollars buy?"

"Not much," Gladys said. "We've already checked the catalogues. A couple of gold rings, that's about it. I still say a cheque would be best. We could get Jeremy to write us one."

"Too risky," Mabel said. "And possibly dishonest, too. In any case, we have only about four hundred and fifty dollars left, after we pay Jeremy.

"We have an outstanding bill with a mail-order company that we would like you to pay for us," Mabel went on. "Our package should be arriving today."

"What did you order?"

"Oh ... hats, that sort of thing ...," Dotty said vaguely.

"I don't plan to hang around here all day just to receive your deliveries," I said.

"Oh, you don't have to," Gladys said. "We have it all figured out. Just leave the door unlocked, and when the delivery truck arrives we'll sing out for them to leave our parcel in the front hall. I can snag it from the couch with my umbrella handle if I lean way out and the others hold me. We can set out the money in an envelope."

"Run along and enjoy yourselves now," Dotty said. "Don't worry about us. We'll manage."

"And never mind about the gold," Mabel added. "I have learned from long experience not to expect much from money. It is far better to rely upon one's wits rather than upon the things we hope money will do for us. Put it back in the couch, please."

I did.

"Thank you," Mabel said. "And now, goodbye, and — behave yourselves."

"Yes, don't do anything we wouldn't do," Gladys said. "So long, boys. Toodle-oo ..."

"Goodbye, dear friends. We'll miss you." Dotty blew us a kiss, and got out her handkerchief and dabbed her eyes.

I thought they were just being sarcastic.

Chapter Four

THE AUNTIES MUTINY

RICK AND I MET Mark and Scooter at the tennis courts and whumped them in three sets of doubles. It was great. Afterwards we went over to the ball diamond. There was a benefit game at two and they were giving out free hot dogs. Halfway there, Rick remembered he had a dental appointment at two.

"I'll bike by your place on my way home and pick up my video camera," he said. "I forgot it." He winked at me and biked off.

Sometimes it was fun having a secret the other kids didn't know. After the ball game I stopped at the library and borrowed six books about TV for the aunties. If they were busy reading, they wouldn't be bothering me. I got home around five.

"Hi, Jeremy," my mom said. "How was your day?"

"Pretty good."

"What did you do?"

"Oh, nothing much." This is a typical conversation between me and my mom. "How was yours?"

"Exhausting!" Her shoulders slumped. "Cleaning up that old theatre is more work than any of us thought. I'm looking forward to a relaxing evening — no cooking. I'll just nuke some dogs, then we can flop in front of the tube."

My stomach turned over at the thought of more hot dogs. I had eaten six at the ball park. "Don't worry about me — I'll make my own supper," I said, "and since when do you 'flop in front of the tube'?"

"There's a nature show on at seven about wild orangutans. It sounds interesting."

On my way up to the bathroom I went into the living room and set the library books on the coffee table. Something looked different. I suddenly realized what. I could see the couch — the aunties weren't on it! I looked around. All that was left of them was the stuff they'd cleaned out of their purses, and a large empty box marked "Aeronautical Supplies, Toronto."

Aeronautical Supplies? Was this the mail-order parcel they'd been waiting for? What had been in the box? Had they ordered a collapsible glider and flown off on some adventure without me? They'd been acting very strange, now that I thought about it — the way they'd said goodbye and everything. To think they would go somewhere without me! Without even telling me! It was totally — rude! I couldn't believe it. Never trust an auntie, I reminded myself. They are full of tricks and bad surprises. Maybe the box contained a helicopter kit that they had put together and — no, the box wasn't nearly big enough. But what about a hot-air balloon? Was that why they'd been so busy cleaning their purses — so there'd be no extra baggage to weigh them down? I ran out the front door and gazed up into the sky. Nothing but clouds and a thick white jet stream. What had I expected to see? The aunties holding onto their hats, waving their handkerchiefs from a basket swinging below a big striped balloon? I went back inside, feeling stupid. The aunties could barely move and they certainly couldn't walk. How could they get into a balloon basket, push themselves out through the front door, fire up the gas jets, and drift away on a journey without any help? It was ridiculous. Anyway, the box wasn't that big, and whatever was in it had cost them only a hundred and fifty dollars.

That meant someone had moved them. I ran back to the kitchen. "The aunties are missing!" I told my mom.

"I know."

"Did you take them? To the theatre, to use in one of your plays?"

"No, not yet," she said. "I still think it's a good idea, though. Three old ladies whose only job is to sit there watching the other actors. They would never speak or react — just sit and watch. A sort of mute audience right on stage. What a scream!"

"Who took them, then?"

"I thought you did."

"Why would I kidnap my own aunties?"

"What are you talking — kidnapping?"

"Well, they're missing," I said. "Someone must have taken them, right? I mean, they couldn't get up and walk out."

It occurred to me that the delivery person who had dropped off the aeronautical box might have seen the aunties on the couch and stolen them, thinking they were rare art objects or something. But that idea was pretty far-fetched. Delivery people would be prime suspects, and wouldn't be stupid enough to steal stuff the same day they made a delivery. Besides, judging from the rest of our house, they would know there wasn't likely to be any valuable art in it.

"Who would steal stuffed dolls?" my mother asked. "If we report it to the police, will they take us seriously? Would it be considered theft or missing persons?" She laughed. "Rick probably borrowed them."

I quickly checked the living room to see if Rick's video camera was still there. It wasn't. Which meant he must have come by. OR — whoever had taken the aunties had taken the camera too.

"Jeremy," my mother said, "you're dancing up and down like a puppet on a string. If you have to go to the bathroom, please, go."

I went.

My mom was probably right. Rick had probably taken the aunties. He wasn't as used to their tricks as I was. He'd be like Play-Doh in their hands. If they wanted to go on a

47

little bike ride, or see what his house looked like, they'd be able to talk him into it in five minutes. He wasn't as experienced at saying no as I was. I felt a little upset that the aunties might prefer his company to mine, though. Just because we'd had a couple of arguments was no reason for them to leave without a word.

I dialled Rick's number.

"Howdy, stranger. Ricketts here," drawled his answering machine. "I'm not around the ranch right now, but I'll be back after sundown. So long, partner. Giddap, Jewel." A horse whinnied and hoofbeats faded into the distance.

"It's Jeremy," I said, after the beep. "I suppose you've got the aunties. I suppose they wanted to see what someone else's house looked like. Or see what it was like to spend the night. Call me when you get back. 'Bye."

I wondered if he was out somewhere with the aunties, or if he'd gone out alone, leaving them at the mercy of that yappy little Solange. I decided not to waste any more time worrying about them. They hadn't even bothered to leave me a note. Well, if they were going to run away behind my back, they could just *stay* away for a while. Rick could keep them for a week. Or a month or a year. Let them run someone else's life. They would beg to come back, but I would make them promise to quit bossing me or no more comfy couch at my place!

I made myself a Jell-O sandwich, and Mom and I played cribbage during dinner. At seven o'clock we went into the living room to watch the orangutan show. I turned on the TV. All I got was black and white fuzz. I flicked around to every channel. It was all the same.

"Don't tell me the TV's broken," Mom said. "Did you disconnect something when you hooked up that VCR? I knew I shouldn't have let you buy that thing. You watch too much as it is. There's so much junk out there, and someone your age doesn't have the ability to judge what's good and what's garbage. If you broke something, you can pay to have it fixed yourself. I'm going upstairs to read in the tub. By the way," she added, as she left the room, "have you seen my radio hat around? Did you borrow it?"

"Are you kidding?" The hat she was talking about was a straw safari hat with a metal point on top that you could pull an antenna out of. Inside the hat was a little radio with batteries and earphones. It looked totally weird.

"What's wrong with it? I happen to like it. I'm going to be alone at the theatre tomorrow, since it's Saturday, and I thought I'd paint better if I could tune in some music." She went upstairs.

I flicked the TV on and off a few times. Usually my mom was as critical of TV as the aunties, so you'd think she'd be glad it was broken. But why blame me? I hadn't done anything. I fiddled around with the remote control. The black and white fuzz gradually turned into shapes and became clearer. At first I thought I saw three orangutans sitting side by side. I was just about to call Mom when the picture became more distinct and I realized that they weren't orangutans at all. They were three women wearing helmets and goggles. I looked more closely. They were! They were Mabel, Gladys, and Dotty! My heart skipped a beat. I flicked through all the channels. The aunties were on every one. Maybe the remote control was broken.

Then I nearly laughed out loud as I realized what must have happened. When Rick had stopped by to pick up his camera, the aunties must have talked him into making a video of them after all. Okay, it was a pretty good joke, I had to admit. But if they thought Rick could make a better movie of them than I could, they were wrong. It was the most boring video I'd ever seen. The aunties just sat on the couch, talking as usual. They looked a little camera-shy, as if they were nervously waiting for something important to happen. And they looked pretty ridiculous in their helmets — they were leather pilots' helmets with a strap under the chin and goggles attached. Long scarves were draped around their necks. So that was what had come from the aeronautical company.

"How long do you suppose it's going to take?" Dotty was asking.

"Patience, dear," said Mabel. "This is rather different from what I expected, I confess, but I do not expect it will last long."

"I think it's a big fat yawn," Gladys said. "Whose idea was this, anyway?"

"We all agreed to do it," Dotty said. "For goodness' sake, we mustn't go blaming one another. It's good to try new things, even when we don't know what the outcome will be. That's what keeps us young at heart."

"My helmet's too tight," Gladys grumbled.

I had forgotten how comfortable the couch was. I stretched out full length and wiggled my toes. It sure was a lot softer than the floor. I must have dozed off. When I woke up it was morning and the aunties video was still on. I flicked off the TV, got myself a bowl of Swheatios, and biked over to Rick's.

Rick's dad, Professor Ricketts, let me in. Rick was still sleeping, so I had a second breakfast of leftover Chinese food with his dad while I waited. My fortune cookie said: "You will soon take an interesting trip."

Great! I thought. I hadn't been anywhere in ages. Maybe Mom would rent a cottage at the lake for a week.

Rick appeared in the doorway. "Hi. What are you doing here so early?"

"It's quarter to nine," I said.

"Is it?" Professor Ricketts exclaimed, glancing at the clock. "I'd better run."

When he was gone, I said, "Where were you last night? I phoned about the video and got your Lone Ranger recording. How come you never called back?"

"I was shopping for cowboy boots. It was late when I got home. What video?"

"The video you made of the aunties. How did you convince them to let you film them?"

"I never made a video of the aunties."

"Oh, come on," I said. "Where are you hiding them? In your room?"

"The aunties? I haven't seen them since yesterday. What — are they missing?" He really didn't seem to know.

"You mean you don't have them? But where — ? Wait a minute," I said. "Yesterday, when we were going to the ball park, you left for a dental appointment. What happened after that?"

"I went by your place, picked up my camera, dropped it off here, brushed my teeth, and went to the dentist's."

"And were the aunties at my place when you picked up your camera?"

"Of course. Where else would they be? They got me to bring their box in from the hall and asked me to lock the door on my way out."

"And did you?" I asked.

"Yes. What's the big mystery?"

"When I got home, the aunties were gone. I thought you'd taken them. There's no way they could get away on their own — unless they've been lying all this time about not being able to walk."

"You think someone *stole* them?" Rick asked.

"But you locked the door — and it didn't look as if anyone had broken in. Anyway, that still doesn't explain the video. It was in my VCR last night. If you didn't make it, who did? It must have been made *before* you picked up your camera. And the aunties disappeared *after* you left. It doesn't make sense. I mean, whoever took that video of them didn't do it against their will. They acted perfectly normal — as if it was just another day on the couch. They weren't upset or anything."

"Maybe the aunties took a movie of themselves," Rick suggested.

"No way," I said. "They'd have had to get off the couch to reach the camera, and even then it would be too heavy for them to lift."

"Why don't we go back to your place and watch the video," Rick suggested. "It might give us some clues. I'll just grab some breakfast first. Hey! You ate my sweet and sour pork! *And* my fortune cookie! I was saving that."

"Sorry. Here's the fortune." I handed it over.

"'You will soon take an interesting trip,'" he read. "Well, that's true, anyway. I leave for Calgary at three this afternoon."

"But I've got to find the aunties! I need your help."

"We've got about six hours," Rick said. "Five, really, because I haven't packed yet."

"Let's go," I said. "We'll check the video for clues and then decide what to do. Come on."

Chapter Five

AIR THIEVES!

WE BIKED BACK TO my place at full speed. I turned on the TV. There were the aunties, in black and white, wearing their pilots' helmets and goggles and chatting about knitting stitches.

"I prefer the stocking stitch myself," Mabel was saying. "A nice, durable, no-nonsense stitch that gives a plain, tidy look. Why, some of these fancy new patterns have so many dropped stitches they might as well be crochet."

"I'm rather partial to crochet work," Dotty said in an offended voice.

Gladys, between them, was clumsily knitting what looked like the beginning of a scarf. Her forehead was wrinkled in concentration.

"Oh, I suppose crochet has its place," Mabel replied. "As a border on handkerchiefs and pillow slips. But when it comes to knitting, the stocking stitch is —"

Rick had been squatting beside the TV, watching. All at once he got up and said, "There's no video in the VCR slot, Jeremy."

"What do you mean, no video?" I went over and pressed the EJECT button. Nothing came out of the slot. I stuck my hand in. Sure enough, it was empty.

"But, but —" I said. "How can a video be playing when there's nothing in the machine?" I flicked the dial around to every channel. Nothing changed on the screen. The aunties were still arguing about knitting.

"And the aunties are missing ...," Rick said slowly. "What does that tell you?"

"I don't know. What? What *does* it tell me?"

"It's obvious, isn't it?" Rick said. "The aunties are on TV."

"The aunties? On TV? But how could they have got to a TV studio? Who would have taken them?" A thought struck me. "Do you think they're on *everybody's* TV or just on this one?"

"That's easy to find out," Rick said. "We can bike back to my place and check."

We went out the back door.

"Just a second." Rick bent down to pick up the newspaper. It comes early on Saturday. He flipped to the local section.

"Uh-oh. Take a look." He pointed to a short article on page three.

TV BLACKOUT A MYSTERY

An unexplained technical problem left the city without television last night. Staff at C-KIT, an affiliate station

56

of the national network C-CAN, were unable to find a reason why stations were prevented from broadcasting for over six hours to press time. For determined viewers one show was available, a poor-quality black-and-white documentary of three seniors discussing life.

My hands were shaking. I leaned against the wall and read it again.

"The whole city?" I said. "Not just my TV?"

"Looks like it," Rick said. "Awesome."

"I knew the aunties were up to something," I said. "But this! It's unbelievable! We've got to think about it. We've got to do something. We need a plan."

We went back inside and flicked on the TV again. The aunties were still wearing their helmets, but they had shoved the goggles up on their heads. They were discussing whether criminals should get out of jail early for good behaviour.

"I can't believe they're doing this!" I said. "Traitors! After we kept their secret all summer, now they're going public and letting the whole world know they can speak. Who did they talk into helping them get on TV?"

The fact was, I couldn't imagine anyone breaking into my living room and taking the aunties to some secret studio where they could mess up every TV station. I tried to think of some logical explanation — although, knowing the aunties, it didn't have to be logical. Maybe they had been kidnapped by aliens and were now orbiting the earth, interfering with satellite broadcasting. Maybe Rick had secretly made a really long video which he somehow managed to get on the air, had hidden the aunties somewhere, and was now planning to escape to Calgary, leaving me to take the blame.

I stared at him. "You didn't have anything to do with this, did you?" I asked. I used to be a very trusting person. Living with the aunties had made me suspicious.

"Of course not," Rick said. "I don't know any more than you do."

"You knew there was no video in the VCR."

"Anybody could see that. You should have noticed yourself, last night."

"I was tired," I said. "I didn't think to check."

"There's only one TV studio in town, isn't there?" Rick asked. "The aunties must be there. But who took them?"

"And why are the TV people letting them go on and on?" I asked. "Are they barricaded in a room somewhere so no one can get at them?"

"Maybe they're *not* at the studio," Rick said. "If they're on every channel, how can they be broadcasting from the studio? Besides, if they were at the studio, it would have been in the newspaper article, wouldn't it? I know, maybe they're at a cable company!" He glanced at his watch. "It's nearly eleven. We don't have much time before I have to leave. That leaves us about three hours. If we split up we can do twice as much. Why don't you check out the TV studio and I'll check the cable company." He thought for a minute. "If we do find the aunties, how are we going to get them back here?"

"They're used to bikes," I said. "I've driven around two or three times with them strapped to my bike."

"What if they don't want to come?" he asked. "They look very calm. Almost as if they're enjoying themselves."

I looked at the screen.

"I do feel that if prisoners behave like gentlemen for five years, or say ten," Dotty said, "they should get out early. Unless they've murdered someone or done something really dreadful."

"Gentlemen?" Mabel asked. "Are you implying that all criminals are men?"

"No," said Gladys. "Just most of them."

"I see no reason why they should get out early for good behaviour," Mabel said. "Anyone can behave oneself in prison. It is one's duty."

"I heard that it costs more money to keep prisoners in jail than to keep old people in nursing homes," Gladys said. "It takes big bucks to pay for guards and barbed wire and alarms. Not to mention food and TVs and university courses."

"I say they should all be on bread and water," Mabel said. "Every man jack of them. They should have to work for a living like everyone else, not lounge about on the public purse. There's plenty of garbage to be picked up, and roads to be built and snow to be shovelled."

"They could all be dumped on an island in the Arctic," Gladys said. "Plenty of snow to shovel, and they wouldn't need guards. They could build themselves igloos, and a plane could drop off groceries once a month or so."

Dotty shivered. "I can't imagine the prisoners *we* know on an island in the Arctic, can you? Harpooning seals? Stalking walruses?"

"They're talking about the Banks Brothers!" Rick exclaimed.

"We've got to find them before they say something that will get us into trouble," I said. "We're bringing them back whether they want to come or not!"

"If I took a rope along, I bet I could lasso them," Rick said. "I've been practising up for the wild west, in case there's a contest at the Stampede."

I went out to the garage and returned in a minute with a length of rope for Rick and an old volleyball net for myself. "Let's go get them!" I said.

We set off, me pedalling as fast as I could on my old bike to keep up with Rick's ten-speed.

At the laundromat on King Street we went our separate ways, agreeing to meet back at Rick's at one-thirty. That would give us over two hours. Rick's job was to explore the cable-television building. My job was to check out the television studio. If either of us found the aunties, we would load them onto our bike and take them to Rick's.

It took me about ten minutes to reach the C-KIT studio. To my surprise there was a small crowd on the sidewalk in front of the building, and a policeman guarding the front door.

Wow! This was more serious than I'd thought. I chained my bike to a hydro pole down the block and joined the crowd.

"We're paying good money to get thirty-three channels," a big man near me shouted at the cop. "How dare they cut it down to one?"

"We won't have our viewing dictated!" a woman yelled. "We demand freedom of choice!"

Someone started a chant that was taken up by everyone — including me, since I didn't want to stick out of the crowd. It went:

> C — K — I — T
> Give us choice on our TV.
> C — K — I — T
> Give up your monopoly!

We chanted this about five times. I wasn't sure what "monopoly" meant; I thought it was a game. But no one seemed to be having much fun. Eventually the chant died down and I found myself shouting, "C — K —" only to realize I was the only one. I slipped behind the big man.

The cop came down the steps towards the group and said, "I understand your concern, folks. I wasn't real happy about missing the ball game last night either. But break it up now and head along home. C-KIT will have their wires uncrossed just as soon as they can. They want to get the problem cleared up as much as you do. Move along now."

How was I going to get in there? I explored the outside of the building and found two other doors, but neither of them opened from the outside — they didn't even have doorknobs. It looked as though you needed to stick a special card in a slot to make them open. I made my way around to the front door. The cop was still there.

I decided I needed some food. I think better on a full stomach, and it was close to lunchtime anyway. I dug into my shorts pockets and came up with a loonie and eighty-seven cents, enough for a burger and ginger ale at the fast-food place up the street. Sure enough, after just one bite of my burger, I had a brainwave. I wrapped up my food and headed back towards C-KIT.

"No one's allowed in here without a pass," the policeman said as I marched up the steps to the studio.

I held up my burger and pop. "Then how about you take this in and deliver it to the short guy with glasses and freckles in studio two? He's hungry. I'll watch the door while you're gone."

(I was describing myself, of course. *I* was the short hungry guy with glasses and freckles who planned to be in

studio two in a few minutes — if there was a studio two —
and if my plan worked.)

The cop looked doubtful. "Don't they have a cafeteria
in there?"

I shrugged. I had no idea.

"Okay then, take it in to him, but make it snappy.
When you come out again maybe you can nip around the
corner and pick up a coffee and doughnut for me, eh?"

"No problem," I said, as he opened the door.

Inside the dim lobby, a nasal voice said, "N-yes?"

A woman with a black and blonde brushcut, and a plastic tube running from her ear to her mouth, was looking at
me across a large reception desk.

"Uh, hi." I waved and edged past her desk, making for
a glass door that seemed to be the only way in.

"May I n-help you?" she asked, in a very unhelpful
tone of voice.

I held up the food again. "The policeman outside the
door said I'm supposed to take this to studio two and make
it snappy."

She glared at me. "Who wants it?"

"Uh — a short guy with glasses and freckles?"

The phone rang. I was about to sneak through the door,
but she pointed a long purple fingernail at me and I froze.
She carried on a brief conversation through her plastic tube.

"No unauthorized persons past this point," she said as
she hung up.

"The burger's getting cold," I said. "And the pop's getting warm."

"I'll have someone deliver it." She pressed a few buttons and spoke into her tube again.

"No one's available," she said. "They're all in a meeting. You can leave it with me."

But —" I said, "but —"

The phone rang again. The receptionist pushed a button and began to talk.

"There he is!" I cried, pointing at my reflection in the glass door. Before the receptionist could stop me, I pushed open the door and ran.

Chapter Six

INSIDE C-KIT

I RACED DOWN A long, carpeted hall, expecting to be grabbed at any moment by ten long purple fingernails. Suddenly I saw a door marked "Studio 2." I slipped inside. The studio was huge and, fortunately, empty. I recognized the table and armchairs — I had seen them on the evening news, but they looked a lot shabbier in real life. It was cool to be right there in the middle of the news set, as if I were part of the news myself. Which I would be, I reminded myself, if I got caught. No one seemed to be following me, though.

I looked around for a hiding place where I could sit down and eat my lunch. The room was full of sets and curtains, platforms on wheels, and fake scenery. A brand-new red mini-van with tinted windows was parked in a corner. The door was unlocked, so I slipped inside and finished my burger in peace. The ginger ale fizzed all over me when I opened it. My T-shirt got soaked.

I was feeling around for something to wipe my hands on when I heard voices. I looked out the van window and saw the studio door opening. Four people came in. With my heart racing, I locked the doors and crouched down behind the driver's seat. Two of the people rolled up big cameras on wheels and began filming the other two, a man and a woman who sat down and started gabbing about transportation from horse-and-carriage days up to the present. The van was getting hotter and stuffier by the minute, and I had no way out. I could be stuck there for hours. I could suffocate in there! It was the aunties' fault; they were always getting me into sticky situations.

Someone rattled the van door. I looked up, terrified — I had been caught in the act. Then I remembered the tinted windows. They couldn't see me. The cameras were pointed right at the van and the woman was saying, "The vehicle of choice for today's family is of course the minivan." She gave the door a couple of yanks. Her smile disappeared.

"Cut," called a cameraman. "Who's got the keys?"

They walked around the van, trying all the doors. I slid to the floor, sweating.

"This is just great," fumed the woman.

"So we don't film the van. So what?" the cameraman said. "It's not like anyone's out there watching. Let's take another lunch. They should give us the day off."

"Hey, maybe these are the keys," said the man. I slid farther down, trying to squeeze myself under the seat, as I heard the clinking of keys against the lock. A ginger-ale burp was rising in my throat.

"No, these don't work. Let's go talk to George. He'll

have a spare set." There was a mumble of agreement and all four of them left.

I let out a belch of relief, and got out of the van. I gulped in the cool air and mopped my sweaty face with my sticky T-shirt. When I opened the studio door a crack and looked out, the coast was clear. I dashed down the hall.

If the aunties were in the building, they had to be in the main control room, wherever that was. You'd think the TV people would have found them by now. They were either well hidden, or locked in where no one could get at them. It should have been easy enough to cut their power supply, though, and get them off the air that way.

The C-KIT studio had three floors. I checked the remaining rooms on the main floor; two of them were studios, smaller than the first one but also empty, and the other six had a window near the door so I could check them without going in. Most of the rooms were full of computers and TV screens and lots of little glowing coloured lights.

Next I checked the top floor. All the rooms up there were offices. Through one office window I could see four short guys with freckles and glasses eating their lunch. They were laughing and joking, and I felt like going in and asking them if they knew anything about the old ladies jamming the airwaves. I decided not to. There was a washroom too, which I slipped into, and washed the ginger ale off as best I could.

I went down two flights of stairs to check the basement, and nearly walked into the middle of a bunch of people in the cafeteria. I managed to slip behind a post before anyone saw me. They were talking about the aunties.

"We've had thirty-two calls from sponsors wondering about cancelled commercials," the receptionist said, waving her purple nails. "And four hundred and twenty-one calls from the public wondering what's going on."

"It's an outrage," said a man in a grey suit. "We're losing money every second we're off the air."

It sounded as if the workers at C-KIT weren't any surer than I was about what was going on. I was starting to think that it was a dumb idea to suppose the aunties were here at all.

"Whoever is behind this is going to be facing a big lawsuit," another man said. "The networks will be seeing them in court."

Lawsuit? Court? I shivered. If the aunties ended up in prison, I might too! I *had* to find them. I slipped past the cafeteria and into another hallway. The first room was the newsroom, full of people talking on the phone or typing on computers. The next door was open to a big room lined with shelf after shelf of film reels and cassettes, like a huge film library. The last door was marked DO NOT ENTER. But no one was looking, so I turned the knob and cautiously pushed the door open. Wires and cords and pipes and broken cameras and tools and lots of things I didn't know the names of were piled everywhere. It was a long room, with lots of corners and cupboards and aisles and places to hide. It was just the sort of place the aunties might be. I picked an aisle and began creeping down it, glancing into cupboards and under counters as I went. After a while I got bolder and moved faster, since no one seemed to be there.

As I came to the end of the aisle I saw her. It was Mabel, slumped across a desk, half hidden by a file cabinet. I could see the back of her navy suit and a bit of grey hair under the leather helmet squashed down over her head. Gladys and Dotty were probably just around the corner.

"*Psst,*" I whispered. "*Hey, Mabel!*"

There was no response except a small quiver of her back, which I might have imagined.

Had someone knocked her out? Or was someone sitting next to her making sure she didn't speak? If only I could see around the corner. Very carefully, without making a sound, I slipped off my backpack and took out the volleyball net. Crawling along on all fours, I sneaked closer, then popped up and looked around the corner. Mabel was alone. I threw the net over my shoulder and flung it forward. It fell completely over her. "Gotcha!" I cried, pulling it tight.

Mabel threw off the net and leapt to her feet. She *can* move after all, I thought in terror. I gasped as she turned to face me.

But the person looking at me wasn't Mabel. It was a

small, grey-haired security guard in a navy uniform and leather-trimmed hat.

"Sorry," I stammered. "Sorry to disturb your nap. I — I was just trying to catch you and uh — take you home. I — I thought you were someone else. I — I'll just take my net and leave."

He stared at me, eyes popping with fear, as if I were a terrorist or a lunatic. He edged towards a red box on the wall. When he pushed it, alarms began ringing all over the building. I grabbed my net and ran.

I ran as fast as I could, heading for the stairs and bounding up them two at a time. I wasn't sure where to go — the front door didn't seem like a good idea, and the other doors might not open without more alarms going off. Maybe I had some crazy idea that I'd find stairs to the roof and escape that way. Then I remembered the washroom on the top floor. I raced for it — thinking I could lock myself in a cubicle and not be found? I don't know what I was thinking.

I reached the washroom, out of breath. It was empty, to my relief. My mind was going so fast and crazy that when I saw the open window I didn't think twice, just hung my volleyball net on the hook-thing that locked it, gave a couple of tugs to make sure it would hold, and climbed out. I felt like a soldier climbing a rope down the side of the building. I just hoped the net would hold my weight — it was pretty ragged from being left out in the rain a lot.

I got down as far as the first-floor windows before I ran out of net. It was a long jump but I made it, landing in the alley with only a couple of sore heels to slow me down. I didn't want to leave the net hanging there as evidence, but I had no way of getting it, so I just took off. I had to go around to the front of the building to reach my bike. The cop was no longer on the porch; he had probably rushed inside when the alarm went off. He would have to do without his coffee and doughnut. I unlocked my bike and got out of there.

When I finally looked at my watch, I was surprised how much time had passed. I would just have time to get back to Rick's place before he left. How could he leave, right in the middle of things?

His bike was already in his driveway when I got there. I raced in without knocking and found him in his room, throwing clothes into a duffel bag.

"What's up? Any luck?" he asked.

All I could do was pant and puff. Finally I got my breath back. "No sign of them. And I nearly got caught. What about you?"

"Nothing," Rick said. "Saturday is pretty quiet at the cable company. The kindergarten teacher's husband works there. He gave me a tour of the building. Apparently having the same show on every channel doesn't affect the cable company unless people start cancelling their subscriptions because of it. I don't think the cable company has anything to do with it. What did you find out?"

I gave Rick a summary of my adventure at the TV studio, describing how I'd got past the cop, hidden in the van, netted the security guard, and escaped out the bathroom window.

"Some people have all the fun," he said.

"Fun? I bet it took at least six months off my natural lifespan," I said. "I bet my heart used up at least half a year of beats. We've got to find the aunties, Rick. The TV people were talking about lawyers, and court! We could be in major trouble."

"Not me," Rick said. "I'll be in Calgary." He slung his bag over his shoulder. "My mom will be here in fifteen minutes. She's never late."

"What am I going to do?" I realized I was wringing my hands. It hurt. "I need help," I said. "How can I get the aunties back all by myself?"

"Yesterday you wanted to get rid of them," Rick reminded me.

"Well, now I want them back," I said. "I don't want to be sued by the TV networks. I'd lose for sure. Mom would kill me."

"Wherever the aunties are," Rick said, "they must have had help. But who else knows they exist? Besides," he added, "your mother ..."

"Not Mom!" I cried. "She doesn't even know they can talk, I'm positive."

"What if she overheard them and thought she could make some money off them by getting them a show?" Rick asked.

"I — I can't believe it. Mom wouldn't do a thing like that."

"Where has she been lately?" Rick asked, suspiciously. "I haven't seen her around much."

"Working. At the theatre."

"I thought it closed. I thought she lost her job there."

"Yes, but she and her friends got together and bought the building themselves," I explained. They're remodelling it and turning it into a dinner theatre. She's been painting there all week."

"That's what she *says*," Rick said.

"I believe her!" I shouted.

Rick grinned. "Don't worry. I took a minute and biked by the theatre myself, just to check. She was in there painting, like you said."

"You should have trusted her." But I was secretly glad that he'd checked up on her. It was a relief to know she wasn't involved.

"Well, we agree the aunties couldn't have done this alone," Rick said. "So who else knows about them?"

"Just you, me, and my mom," I said. "And all the people Mom invited to her party when she first made the aunties. That includes your dad, Dr. Suggs, and her theatre friends. That's all."

"You're sure nobody else ever saw the aunties?" Rick asked.

I thought hard. "Well, there is Rose, who owns the old-clothes shop where we bought their outfits ... Oh, and a guy who delivered pizza once. And maybe the delivery person who dropped off the aunties' helmets and goggles. As far as I know, no one else has seen them — not even the neighbours."

"What about those two cops?" Rick asked.

"Yikes!" I cried. Constable Rodney Heaves and Constable Sheila Barflie had seen the aunties at least twice. They had been on the scene when we captured the Banks Brothers in our living room. And again when they brought us the reward cheque for capturing the —

I turned to Rick, and gasped, "THE BANKS BROTHERS!"

Chapter Seven

ALL ALONE

"OH MY GOSH, are we in trouble!" I whispered.

"*You're* in trouble. I'll be gone," Rick reminded me.

"But the Banks Brothers are safely locked up in jail," I said. "They *can't* be involved."

"Unless they've escaped," Rick said. "Escaping is their speciality."

"We'd have heard about it on the news," I said.

Rick pointed to the TV. "What news?"

"I'm going to check the newspaper the minute I get home," I said. "But even if the Banks Brothers did escape, why would they kidnap the aunties? Why wouldn't they just rob another bank? It doesn't make sense."

"Revenge?" Rick suggested. "It was the aunties and us who got them captured."

"But — but why put them on TV?"

"Maybe it's some weird kind of videotaped ransom note?" Rick said. "Maybe they can't write."

I shook my head. "Too unbelievable." But I nervously added the names Eddy, Mort, and Harvey Banks to the list of people who knew about the aunties.

"Well, all those people are suspects," Rick said. "And

even if they didn't help the aunties get on TV, they're still a big danger to you."

"What do you mean, a danger?"

"Obviously, any of those people could see the aunties on TV and know they belong to you and your mom. If they report you, well, let's just say it might be a loooooong time before I see you again."

I shivered. The doorbell rang.

"Adios, partner" he said.

"Wait, Rick, just a minute, what do I do next? I ..."

Rick slung his bag over his shoulder. "I kind of wish I wasn't leaving now. Things are just getting interesting." We went out to the limousine.

"Rick! Wait! When will you be back?"

"Thursday. But I'll phone you in a day or two if I get a chance." He got in the car and rolled down the window. "Be careful, eh?"

"What do you mean?" I asked. But the limo roared off, and I was left standing alone on the curb.

Now there was no one I could talk to about what was going on. Not one single person. And I had no idea what to do next. Slowly I headed home.

When I got there, I checked the newspaper carefully to see if the Banks Brothers had escaped from prison, but found nothing. I hid the section containing the article about the TV blackout. If I was lucky it could be days before my mom heard about it. She had lost her radio hat, and the radio in our old convertible didn't work. The only one we had at home was connected to our tape player. I quickly disconnected the wires to the speaker. But I needed to think of a good story to explain the aunties' absence before Mom realized they were on TV and assumed I had something to do with it. If she knew they'd been stolen, she'd go straight to the police. If the police got involved, they'd have proof that the aunties could talk, and would take them away from me forever. If they didn't put them in jail, they'd probably put them in a museum, or sell them to the circus. I'd never be able to prove I'd had nothing to do with it.

The phone rang. I answered it with a sinking feeling. What now?

"Hello, Jeremy!" a voice said. "Did you know your old dolls are on TV?"

"Who — who is this?" I murmured, beginning to shake.

"Dr. Suggs. I just turned on the TV, and what do I see but the three dolls your mother made for that party. It's great! They're hilarious. How did they get them to talk in such a realistic way? Is your mother home? Can I speak to her?"

"No."

He laughed. "No she's not home, or no I can't speak to her?"

"You can't speak to her because she's not here," I said. I

took a breath and decided to bluff it. "What are you talking about — dolls on TV?"

"Yes, you know those dolls your mother made? Well, I just turned on channel thirteen and there they were, saying all kinds of nasty things about the prime minister. It was too funny, coming from these three old girls! I'm amazed they got away with that on the air."

I was dying to know what the aunties had said, but I told Dr. Suggs he must be mistaken. I reached over and turned on the TV so I wouldn't be lying when I added, "The dolls are right here in my living room. I'm not sure what you've got on your TV, but it's got nothing to do with me and Mom. Didn't you know there's some kind of TV problem? On every channel. All over the city."

"Is that so? No, I never heard. Well, they certainly *look* like your mother's old dolls. Of course, I was a little, er, under the weather at that party, so I could be mistaken. Yes, now that I look more closely, I can see that these puppets only slightly resemble your dolls. In fact, they look a lot more like real people than puppets. Actually, I suppose they *are* real people, with stocking masks pulled over their faces to distort their features. Oh well, my mistake, I guess. But it's always nice to talk to you, Jeremy. Say hello to your mother for me. Goodbye."

I breathed a sigh of relief and flopped onto the couch. *That* was a close one. I reached for the remote control and turned up the TV volume. The aunties had stopped talking about the prime minister and were now discussing casseroles.

"Ooh," Gladys said, with a faraway look in her eyes, "how well I remember the delicious smell of chicken pot pie simmering in the Dutch oven. Biting through that flaky crust into the rich, juicy gravy and succulent morsels of meat and carrots. Mmmmm mmm."

My stomach started growling. It had been ages since Mom had made anything that good.

"My favourite was always deep-dish macaroni and cheese," Dotty said. "I loved that creamy cheese sauce, and the crispy topping of golden cracker crumbs and bits of bacon."

My mouth began to water.

"I was partial to toad-in-the-hole as a child, myself," Mabel said. "All those tasty little sausages popping out of the egg and cheese soufflé. It would melt in your mouth."

"Hello, I'm home!" The back door slammed. I turned off the TV, just as my mother walked into the living room.

"Hi, Mom. What's for supper?"

"Supper? Oh, I don't know. Leftovers, probably."

"Leftover hot dogs? Ugh."

"Hmm, well, maybe I'll open a can of tomato soup. Or how about mushroom for a change?"

"You know what would be nice," I said, "is if you cooked a real meal for a change. Something like chicken pot pie, or macaroni and cheese, or ..."

"What would be *nice*," she said, "is if certain people, who sit around all day dreaming about food, learned to cook and had something ready when their hard-working mother came home exhausted at night!"

"All I said was —"

"I heard you."

I went out to the kitchen and started setting the table. She joined me a few minutes later.

"Sorry I snapped at you, kiddo," she said.

"How about toad-in-the-hole for supper?" I asked.

"Toad-in-the-hole? You'd never eat it. I remember your reaction that time I made frogs' legs."

"I thought toad-in-the-hole was an egg and sausage dish," I said.

"It is, but how do you know? I've never made it."

"Oh, I, um, heard about it on TV."

"I didn't know you watched cooking shows, Jeremy. You continue to surprise me. By the way, I solved the mystery of why the TV wasn't working last night."

I gulped. "You — you did?"

"Yes, it was very simple. There was something stuck in the video slot. I found it this morning when I went to watch the news before breakfast."

"And uh, d-did you actually see the news?" I stammered.

"As a matter of fact, no," my mother said. "I got sidetracked looking for my radio hat and ran out of time."

I breathed a sigh of relief.

"I'll watch it now, instead," she said.

"Oh, no," I said. "No, I don't feel like TV right now."

"That's a new one, Jeremy. I've never heard you say that before."

"It's just that the evening news is incredibly boring," I said. "I'm sure we can find something better to do."

"I'm sure you're right. Let's watch it anyway, before we eat."

"No!"

"What?"

"No," I said, more quietly this time. "I do not want to watch TV tonight."

She looked at me curiously, then laughed.

"Okay, Jeremy, no one's forcing *you* to watch it, all right? But I had a long day and I feel like vegging out at the moment, if you don't mind. So dinner will be delayed half an hour while I put my feet up and soften my brain."

I raced into the living room ahead of her and stood in front of the TV like a guard.

"What's going on?" She laughed. "What's with the bizarre behaviour?"

"No TV!" I cried. "Not now! Later. There's nothing on now."

"The news is on. Get out of my way, Jeremy. I want to see if I really fixed the TV. I'm quite a handywoman when I put my mind to it, you know."

"There's nothing on, believe me," I protested. "Nothing you'd want to see, honestly."

"I ll be the judge of that. Move over," she ordered.

What could I do? I moved.

She reached out and turned on the TV.

Chapter Eight

NO NEWS IS GOOD NEWS?

I FRANTICALLY TRIED another approach. "Uh, Mom," I said. "I think you'd better sit down. We've got to talk."

I turned the TV off before the aunties materialized out of the grey fuzz, and sat down on the carpet.

"Oh boy," she said, taking a seat on the couch. "How about you talk and I listen?"

"Um," I began, but I could think of nothing else to say.

"Suppose you begin at the beginning," she suggested.

"Oh no," I said, "that would take way too long." I didn't plan to tell her any more than was absolutely necessary.

"Start at the end then," she said.

That was much easier. "There's something on TV I don't want you to see," I began.

"I gathered that," she said. "Hey, young man — you haven't subscribed to one of those adult channels behind my back, have you? Those channels with restricted movies and things? You'd better not —"

"Oh no," I said quickly, "it's nothing like that. I, actually, it's just that ..."

"Well, out with it," she said. "It can't be that bad. Tell

me all about it and I can still catch the last bit of the news."

"That's the point," I said. "You can't see the news."

"Why not? Oh, Jeremy! Don't tell me you got into trouble downtown today and I'm going to see it on the news! Don't tell me you joined some nasty little gang that goes around throwing rocks through plate-glass windows and scrawling bad words on brick walls! Oh, I knew I shouldn't leave you alone all summer like this. I shouldn't have let you talk me out of a babysitter. I should have enrolled you in day camp. I should have brought you along to work where I could keep my eye on you. You could be useful scraping paint and cleaning brushes —"

"Mom, MOM!" I interrupted. "It's not that at all. You can't watch the news because there isn't any news."

That got her attention. "What did you say?"

"There's no news today," I repeated.

"That's what I thought you said. Jeremy, I've been waiting for this for years. Years! The day when the news people would finally catch on to the fact that news doesn't happen on a daily basis. The day they'd finally realize that there are days on which absolutely nothing of any significance whatsoever occurs. The day they'd admit that the so-called news is nothing but stale, recycled misinformation. This in itself is news! This is a great day in television history, son. Quick, turn it on. I want to witness a blank screen for the first and possibly only time. Finally, some truth in broadcasting. No more of this manufacturing of news, this regurgitation of yesterday's story, this rehash of last week's highlight, this trashy sensationalism they pass off as —"

"Mom," I said quietly. "You're missing the point. The TV isn't working."

She stared at me, then heaved a sigh. "Darn," she said. "I knew it was too good to be true." Then she glared at me. "So you're telling me the TV really *is* broken. Well, all I can say, Jeremy, is that this will affect you more than me. I simply can't afford a new TV. Or repairs either. You'll just have to do without. I expect it will be good for you. Maybe you'll learn that electrical appliances are not toys. Maybe you'll learn to amuse yourself instead of relying on mindless shows for entertainment. Maybe you'll —"

"No," I protested, "I didn't break it, I —" I stopped in mid-sentence. It had just occurred to me how convenient it would be if Mom thought the TV was broken. I wouldn't have to tell her about the aunties at all. I felt like laughing, but looked down at the carpet sadly and said, "I'm really sorry — I'll try to get it fixed as soon as possible." I meant it, too.

"There are worse things in life than no TV," she said. "You can always go watch it at a friend's place if you feel withdrawal pains. Come on, how about that toad-in-the-hole you wanted? I'm sure I've got a recipe somewhere."

She went out to the kitchen, whistling. I turned on the TV with the volume low.

"... Boston cream pie with mounds of whipped cream

and shredded coconut on top," Dotty was saying dreamily.

"Triple chocolate-fudge layer cake with mocha icing and rum sauce and a giant scoop of butterscotch ice cream," Gladys said.

I licked my lips.

"What time is it?" Mabel asked.

Gladys pulled the old-fashioned pocket watch from her purse. "Six-fourteen."

"A.m or p.m.?" Mabel asked.

"P.m., of course," Gladys said. "At least, I think it's probably p.m. We've been gone just over twenty-four hours, by my calculations."

"This is taking far longer than I anticipated," Mabel said nervously.

"I wonder if Jeremy's worried about us," Dotty said.

"Yikes!" I exclaimed. They had said my name. Right on TV, for all the world to hear. How long would it take the police to track down all the Jeremys in town? I held my breath as the aunties went on.

"Jeremy won't worry about us," Gladys said. "He knows we're an adventuresome trio."

"I just wish there were some way we could communicate with him." Dotty sighed. "Write him letters and send him birthday greetings and little Christmas packages and so on."

"Pull yourself together, Dotty dear," Mabel said. "You know that is not possible. We weighed all the gains and losses before making this decision, and we cannot go back now."

I leaned forward. This was news. It sounded as though the aunties planned on never coming back at all. As though no one had stolen them or even helped them — as though they didn't even know they were being filmed ...?

"The future will be infinitely preferable to sitting on a couch like dummies, staring at a television all day," Mabel said.

"I miss Jeremy already," Dotty said.

"So why did you leave, then?" I whispered.

"Pull yourself together, Dotty dear," Mabel repeated.

"Yes, we were tired of being toys for a half-grown wiseapple whipper-snapper," Gladys said.

"I wasn't that bad," I said. "Was I?"

"We have more important things to do than decorate his couch," Gladys added. "And listen to him tell us over and over that we can't do anything without him. I guess we showed him!"

"Well, fine," I said. "If that's how you feel, I don't have to listen to you either!" I went over and zapped them out of existence, watching as they faded to a little square in the middle of the TV, and then blinked away entirely. I went out to help with the toad-in-the-hole.

"Were you talking to yourself in there?" my mom asked.

"No," I said.

"I thought I heard you talking to yourself."

"Well, I wasn't," I said.

The toad-in-the hole tasted all right — except for the leftover string beans Mom had added, which had turned sort of grey and looked like worm-in-the-hole. I made a grape Jell-O sandwich for dessert.

After supper Mom settled down to read the paper. "Where's the local section?" she asked. "How do you like that? No local section! Not only does the TV break down, but the newspaper arrives without the local section. *And* I can't find my radio hat! How is a person supposed to know what's going on in this town?"

"No news is good news?" I said.

She snorted.

I waited while she read the part of the paper I hadn't hidden under the couch, and went upstairs. I followed her up, then sneaked back down and turned on the TV again. The aunties had exchanged their helmets for their regular hats, and didn't look quite as much like orangutans now. In fact, they were far more recognizable to anyone who had seen them before. Gladys and Dotty were giggling over a clumsy game of cat's cradle. A length of wool from the scarf Gladys was knitting was arranged around her gloves in a complicated pattern, and Dotty was attempting to pick up the strings and transfer them over to her own limp hands. They found the game very funny, apparently.

"Twiddledy-dee," Dotty giggled. "Twiddledy-dum.

Hope I'm not tickling you, dear."

"No," Gladys said, "but if you don't relax your tension you'll cut off my circulation, ha ha." She waggled her thumbs and flopped them over.

The phone rang. I answered, hoping it was Rick. Maybe he had landed in Calgary already and was calling from the airport. I could tell him the latest and get some advice.

"Jeremy?" said a voice that came from far away.

"Hi, it's me," I said. "Is this you, Rick?" There was a lot of static on the line. Then the voice said, "Hello, sonny. My brothers and me wanted to congratulate you on your show." It was definitely not Rick's voice.

"Who — who is this?" I asked.

"It's me, Eddy Banks, calling long distance from the slammer here in Kingston."

"B-B-Banks?" I stuttered. "You must have the wrong n-n-number."

His loud laugh hurt my ear. "I don't think so. Now listen up, sonny. Me and my brothers have some advice for you, and this call's costing me money, so don't waste my time."

My mind raced with possibilities. How had the Banks Brothers got the aunties if they were still in jail? How had they got them on TV? Were the aunties safe? How could I rescue them without Rick? My thoughts were interrupted by Eddy's threatening growl.

"Me and Mort and Harv seen your show on TV with

them old gals of yours. We don't know what you're up to yet, sonny, but you sure got them TV bigshots fooled. How'd you do it, anyways?"

"Where are they?" I shouted. "I want them back right now, or I'll —"

"Aw, shut it!" he snapped. "You can't fool the Banks Brothers. We know you're behind this scam, and right now it seems we're the only ones with that information — eh? No one else is on to you yet, are they?"

So Eddy Banks thought *I* had put the aunties on TV.

"It's your fault me and my brothers ended up in this pen. You owe us big time, sonny. Here's the deal: we know you collected a reward for our capture. You send us the dough, in small bills, and we won't squeal on you. Sound fair?

"Speak up, sonny, I can't hear you."

"The reward was only a thousand dollars," I said, in a small voice.

"So what? It's the principle of the thing. If we'd known we was going to get caught we'd of turned *ourselves* in and got the reward, see what I mean? That money's ours by rights."

"But I already spent my share on a VCR," I said.

There was a brief silence on the other end of the line; then Eddy Banks said, "Here's what you're gonna do. You're gonna package up that brand-new VCR and mail it special delivery to the Banks Brothers care of the Kingston Penitentiary. We could use our own video machine in here to help pass the time till we bust out. *And* you're going to mail the rest of that thousand bucks to us at the same address. Better yet, send it by courier, it'll be faster. Help pay our phone bills and stuff. Got it?"

"What if I don't?" I whispered.

Eddy Banks laughed a nasty laugh. "If you don't, sonny," he said, "your pal Eddy here will make one little phone call to the chief of police and tell him just who the little brat is that's figured out how to jam the airwaves. You're an air pirate, that's what you are. You know what they used to do with pirates, don't you? Keel-hauled 'em. Planked 'em. Cut out their livers with rusty daggers. Nowadays, of course, they just put 'em in solitary confinement, feed 'em maggoty moosemeat, make 'em scrub floors with their tongues, send 'em to mosquito repellent companies as guinea pigs, give 'em the odd electroshock treatment. Not many survive."

I felt as if I were going to faint.

"So keep your part of our bargain, and I'll keep your little secret. Sound fair?"

In a horrible, hopeless way it did sound sort of fair, but I put on a fake brave voice and said, "I've got nothing to hide. I had nothing to do with the aunties getting on TV."

"Yeah, right." Eddy laughed. "You got till tomorrow night. Twenty-four hours. And then ... ding-a-ling-a-ling ..." I heard a click as he hung up.

I was trembling so much that I dropped the receiver on

the floor with a bang I was sure would bring my mother downstairs. I sat down on the couch and waited to stop shaking.

I had only twenty-four hours. What was I to do? I didn't have Rick's phone number in Calgary, and I couldn't communicate with the aunties. I glanced at the TV. Mabel, who had been staring into the distance, suddenly turned to Dotty and Gladys and said, "Girls, may I have your attention please? I have just had a most dreadful thought."

Chapter Nine

MAROONED IN THE WAVES

GLADYS AND DOTTY looked at Mabel.

"What dreadful thought?" Gladys asked.

"My dears," Mabel said, her voice trembling, "I believe we have made a terrible mistake."

"How so?" Dotty asked nervously.

"I believe," Mabel said, "that we are trapped!"

"Trapped?" Dotty gasped. "What on earth do you mean?"

"We have been here in this strange limbo for approximately twenty-nine hours now," Mabel replied, "ever since the moment we left the living room. Does this not suggest to you a frightening possibility?"

"Do you mean to say we're not going anywhere? Stuff my gullet," Gladys cursed softly. "I sure hope you're wrong, Mabel."

"If we're not getting anywhere," Dotty said, "can't we turn around and go back? I'm tired of this trip anyway. I'm bored and I miss Jeremy."

I cringed. I wished they'd quit saying my name in public like that.

"How *do* we turn around and go back?" Mabel asked.

They looked at each other for several tense minutes.

"Why didn't we think of that before we left?" Gladys asked finally.

"Because we planned never to return," Mabel said. "It never crossed our minds."

"Well, it did cross mine," Dotty said. "I can't really believe we meant never to see dear Jeremy again."

"Believe it," Gladys said grimly. "Looks like we're stuck here, girls, going nowhere fast."

"I have never heard such a frightening thought in my life." Dotty fumbled in her purse for her handkerchief. "I can't, I won't believe it's true."

"That was not actually my dreadful thought," Mabel told them.

"What could be more dreadful than to be trapped in this lonely — nothingness?" Dotty cried.

"I fear," Mabel said, "that we may very likely be, at this precise moment, On Television."

There was a stunned silence.

"What?" I asked the screen. "You mean you didn't *know* you were on TV? You mean someone is secretly filming you — the way Rick and I planned to?"

"What makes you think that?" Dotty asked.

"If you have a more logical suggestion as to where we find ourselves at present, I would like to hear it," Mabel said sharply. "We are no longer in the living room, nor are we at our intended destination. That leaves one possibility, does it not?"

Dotty pressed her handkerchief to her forehead.

"You know, you could be right, Mabel," Gladys said thoughtfully. "Here we are in a place we've never been before ... and it's the most boring place it could possibly be ... it seems very likely that it must be TV. I see it all now — Mabel's right — we must have made a slight miscalculation somehow, and now here we are, stuck on TV!"

"How do I look?" Dotty got out her mirror and rearranged her hair. "Dear me, I've always longed for an audience, and now here I am, unprepared."

"Maybe Jeremy's watching us at this very moment," Gladys said.

I *was* watching, of course — sitting there on the edge of the couch, wondering what the aunties were talking about. It had never occurred to me that they might not know they were on TV.

"So what?" Gladys asked. "Who cares if he's watching or not?"

"Well," Mabel said, "if Jeremy is not watching, he will not know where we are, and if he does not know where we are, how will he be able to help us?"

"Oh, you're so pessimistic tonight, Mabel," Gladys said. "Look on the bright side. We set out on this whole expedition because we were tired of being nothing more than stuffed dolls. We wanted to be live. Well, here we are, live on TV! Yessirree bob!" she continued happily. "This is a dream come true. Just think of it, girls, we can say whatever we like! Do whatever we want! There's no one to stop us! Eeeeeeeeeha!"

"I am going to sing a song," Dotty announced, clasping her gloves to her chin and tilting her head. She began to sing in a high, quavery voice:

"When the moon shines on the ri-hi-ver
And the owl hoots from the tree-hee-hee,
Then my true love comes in my drea-hea-heams
And he speaks these wor-or-ords to me:
Oh my dar-arling, oh my dar-arling, oh —"

"Sit on it, Dotty," Gladys said, "we've got more important things to convey to the public than sentimental little ditties. We can say anything we want. We can even swear if we want to! Oho! I've always wanted to swear in public and get away with it. No one can bleep us out! Dingle-darn!" she yelled. "Get stuffed! Kiss my grits! Eat your patooties! Blow your gizzard to Shanghai! Blow it out your drawers! Ha ha, this is fun. I'll be swashbuckled! I'll be hornswoggled! Chamber pot! Fig face! Shiver my sheets! Take a flying —"

"Gladys!" Dotty cried. "I beg you. Is that any way for a lady to behave in public? Have you no sense of decency?"

"I think I used to have," Gladys chuckled, "but it wore off. Dad bang it! Scorch my timbers! Take a flying —"

"We all know," Mabel said, "that swearing is nothing more than the efforts of a weak mind trying to express itself forcefully."

Gladys laughed loudly. "Who's going to stop me? I've always wanted to say my piece. Here's my big chance. Since it looks as if we're going to be here for a while, let's make the best of it. We all agree TV is a big bore. If we're stuck here on it, we might as well make some changes. Let's ban phoniness first, then we'll ban commercials, then canned laughter. After that we'll make it illegal to end a show on the half-hour. Our shows will end after forty-one minutes, or seventy-seven and a half minutes, or whenever we want them to."

"Oh, Gladys," Dotty said, "you do have some alarming ideas. Do you really think people are watching us?"

"I fear the worst," Mabel said. "Something has gone dreadfully wrong with our plan."

"Since we seem to be stuck here," Gladys went on, "we may as well take our minds off our predicament by scheduling a day of television, aunties-style."

"Oh my — perhaps we could," Dotty agreed. "We could call ourselves ATV — Anti-Television!" She giggled.

"Well," Mabel said, "I suppose we *must* make the best of it. In any case, Jeremy will soon get our note and figure out what happened. There is no sense worrying."

What was that about a note? I hadn't seen a note. I looked around the living room. I checked the coffee table, riffling through the books and magazines in case a note had been slipped inside. I took all the cushions off the couch. I even looked inside the cushions, although I was pretty sure the aunties couldn't open zippers. When nothing turned up, I decided they must mean that they had somehow mailed me a note and that I would be getting it soon.

In the meantime, I had to think of something to do. Obviously I was in danger. The whole city must have heard the aunties use my name by now. The cops would have no trouble finding me. And in twenty-four hours the Banks Brothers would turn me in! What could I do? I didn't have enough information. If this were TV, a helpful clue would come up right about ... now! I waited, but nothing happened. Then I remembered something. My mom had mentioned finding something stuck in the VCR slot. I hadn't asked her what it was. Maybe it was the aunties' note, explaining where they had gone and why. It was a logical place to put a note. They wouldn't have counted on my mother finding it first. Had Mom read it? Had she kept it, or thrown it away?

I turned off the TV and raced upstairs to question her. But she was already asleep, snoring softly. She wouldn't appreciate being shaken awake for a question I couldn't explain. I would have to wait until morning. I decided I might as well get some sleep myself. Tomorrow promised to be a big day, now that I finally had a clue. It would be a relief to have somewhere to start from.

When I got up the next morning, Mom was still asleep. I hoped she would wake up soon so I could ask her what had been in the VCR slot. In the meantime I decided to go over to Professor Ricketts's place to find out if he had a phone number for Rick in Calgary. I left a note for Mom and biked over.

I was glad it was Sunday. On Sunday there was no newspaper delivery. For one more day my mom might not find out about the aunties. I wondered how long it would be possible to keep the news hidden from her. Another day or two? A week? I couldn't hide the newspaper for ever. And one of her friends would certainly phone and tell her soon.

As I biked along, I noticed lots of people out walking and rollerblading and mowing their lawns, or just standing around in groups, talking. It's amazing what people found to do when there was no TV. I had no idea that that many people lived in the neighbourhood.

Professor Ricketts was in his dressing-gown having toast and coffee when I arrived.

"Come in, have a seat, converse," he said, laying aside his book. "This place is so quiet with Rick gone and the TV messed up. I haven't heard a human voice all weekend. Other than my own, talking to the dog. You know, those three women on the TV remind me a lot of those dolls you and your mother made. Don't you think so?"

"Uh — they do look about the same age," I agreed cautiously.

I turned on the TV and flipped the dial around a few times. The aunties were on each channel. Gladys and Dotty were playing a lively game of Snap, and Mabel, hands folded in her lap, looked as though she was quietly thinking. Solange, Rick's poodle, growled at the screen. I turned the TV off.

"What do you think is going on?" I asked. "I mean with the TV. How can someone take over every channel without anyone knowing how they're doing it?"

"It's probably very simple," Professor Ricketts said. "A squirrel probably fell into a transmitter in Mississauga and fried on the wires, just like last year when the power went out. Nothing you can do about these things. No sense calling a repair person. You wouldn't even get through." He buttered his toast, and was just about to take a bite when Solange leaped up and snatched the toast from his fingers.

"Greedy animal!" he said. "That dog will do anything to get toast. She loves it."

"I bet she'd really love French toast," I said.

Professor Ricketts looked puzzled.

"It's a joke," I said. "French poodle, French toast? Get it?" Why is it that as soon as you explain a joke it sounds incredibly stupid?

He put another slice of bread in the toaster.

"I came over to ask if you had Rick's number," I said. "There are a few things I need to ask him." I hoped he wouldn't ask what.

"Unfortunately not," Professor Ricketts said. "But he'll be back in just a few days."

"If he phones you, can you tell him to call me?" I said. "I need to talk to him. It's really important."

I said goodbye to Professor Ricketts, and biked home. I was eager to ask my mom about the note, but halfway home I thought of something that made me pedal even faster. The Banks Brothers had given me a twenty-four-hour deadline to send them the money and the VCR. There were only about ten hours left. Then what? They would turn me in! I could never afford the huge fines I would get for stealing air time. Mom would have to sell the house — even though the bank still owned most of it. We would become street people overnight. It was an interesting idea. Mom wouldn't like it though.

A note was waiting for me on the kitchen counter.

I have walked downtown to buy a Sunday paper. Back soon.

Love, Mom XOXO

Oh no! She would read about the TV problem and demand an explanation. What could I tell her? The fact was, I knew almost nothing about where the aunties were or how they'd got there or why they'd gone. And there was no time to think of an explanation. I had to find a courier company fast, and send off the VCR and all the money I could find. I looked in the yellow pages and dialled the first number I found. It rang four times, then a voice said, "Thank you for calling A1 Courier Systems. We provide quality courier service for all your shipping needs twenty-four hours a day, Monday through Saturday. Please call again during business hours. Thank you. *Click.*"

I dialled another company. "Thank you for calling Ace-Pace Couriers. Our office is open from eight to five Monday to Friday. Please try again. Your call is important to us. *Click.*"

I was about to dial a third company when my mother walked in. It was all over now.

"Hi," I said.

"Why so glum, Jeremy?" she asked. "It's a beautiful day. I've just had a nice walk, and I spent a peaceful half-hour in the doughnut shop reading the paper."

"Go ahead, ask me what it's all about," I said.

"What what's all about?"

"I thought you said you read the paper."

"Only the entertainment section. Why? Is there bad news? An earthquake in Japan? A plane crash in Montreal? A hold-up in Punkeydoodles Corners?"

"No, nothing like that," I said. "So I guess you read

the big entertainment news."

"Yes, I bought *The New York Times* so I could read up on all the Broadway plays and so on. I might get some ideas for our theatre project, you know. It's good to broaden one's reading horizons now and then."

I smiled. New York was light-years away. *The New York Times* wouldn't be reporting on television problems in our little area. I was safe for another day.

I hung around for a couple of hours, trying to phone courier companies without my mom hearing. It wasn't easy. I was in her room using the phone by her bed when she came in and asked who I was calling.

"A-a-a business," I said.

"What business?" she asked.

"My business," I said.

"You don't *have* a business, Jeremy."

"I mean it's my business who I'm calling, not yours."

"Your business is my business when you're using my phone, young man. Don't talk to me like that or I'll find you business that will keep you busy the rest of the day. Like that garage I asked you to clean."

I escaped downstairs. I called all the other couriers in the phone book. Not one was open on Sunday. I hoped the Banks Brothers would understand. I hoped they'd agree to extend my deadline rather than turn me in. I hated giving in to their demands, but I couldn't let them call the police. I felt kind of sick to my stomach. I knew it was nerves.

Maybe my stomach hurt because it needed food. I made myself a shake in the blender out of leftover tea, butterscotch ice-cream, and strawberry jam. It tasted great and made me feel a bit better.

Since Mom was upstairs, I decided to search the rest of the house for her hat — her straw safari hat with the radio and antenna attached. I wanted to find it before she did. I looked in the hall closet, which was quite big, and found lots of interesting things I hadn't seen for a long time. My old stuffed puppy, Arf, was in there. I scratched his head. Why did I always get stuck with stuffed things? Other people had real dogs and real aunts. But I didn't find Mom's radio hat. I checked the coat rack, the kitchen, and finally the garage. The garage was so full of stuff — mainly broken props and sets from Mom's theatre work — that we hadn't been able to keep the car in there for years. The car — that was it! The last time I had seen that hat was on Mom's head when we took the aunties on their first car ride, to the fishing hole. I got the keys, ran out to the driveway, and opened the trunk. There was the hat. I pulled up the antenna, turned on the switch, and stuck it on my head. Nothing. Were the aunties jamming the radio waves too? This was incredible! It took me a few minutes to realize the batteries were dead. I found some new ones in a kitchen drawer and smuggled the hat up to my bedroom to hear the latest.

I tuned in the local station, K900. They weren't playing

the usual top forty hit songs, but were instead interviewing a famous sociologist, Dr. Randolph Skimp.

"This is a social phenomenon with exciting research possibilities," Dr. Skimp was saying. "No modern society would ever, under normal circumstances, agree to completely deprive itself of television for forty hours. How long will the television blackout continue? What will the results be? Will children begin reading books and playing board games again? Or will they take to the streets, bored and angry? Will adults begin to communicate more? Or go to bed earlier? Will the birthrate rise? Will there be demonstrations in the streets? Will droves of citizens mob the movie theatres, unable to live without their favourite form of entertainment?"

"It's not a blackout," the disc jockey said. "You can still get that one channel with those three old ladies talking."

"Correct," said Dr. Skimp. "I believe it is being referred to as a 'grey-out.' Yes indeed — sociologically, those three grey-haired women interest me a great deal. Are they real women, or clever actors mimicking seniors from a bygone era?"

"Thank you, Dr. Skimp. And now, back to our regular music, enthusic, terrusic, bamboozic show!"

I didn't understand half of what Dr. Skimp had said, but the half I did get was a bit scary. What did sociologists actually do? Study televisions?

I took off my hat and turned the dial to the national

station. The daily phone-in show was on.

"Phone toll-free now, and let us know your view of the mysterious television grey-out affecting the entire province," the announcer said.

My mouth fell open. The whole *province*? I thought it was just the city!

Chapter Ten

THE BIG CLUE

LOTS OF PEOPLE called in.

"It's spies!" said one caller. "Some foreign government is trying to create panic. They're trying to sabotage our communication system. It's obviously a political plot!"

"I think radio stations and newspaper owners are behind the TV takeover," another caller said. "When people can't watch TV, they'll listen to the radio a lot more and buy more newspapers and the owners will make more money. That's what's behind it: big money."

"I'm really mad," said a five-year-old named Jody. "I watch TV every single morning, and now I've got nothing to do!"

"I like those three old ladies," said a caller named Sarah. "They're really funny. I like all the jokes they tell, especially the one about the dog named Eileen."

I wondered what joke that was. I must have missed it.

"I'm seventy-two years old," said the next caller. "I'm a widower, attractive, I'm told, and quite well off, and I'd be very interested in meeting those three charming ladies. I enjoy golfing, fine wines, conversation, and I should mention that I drive a Cadillac. A gold Cadillac. I would like to leave my phone number and address so that —"

"Excuse me, sir," said the announcer. "I'm sorry, but we're not running a dating service on this show. Try a newspaper ad. Time for one last call before we go back to our regular programming."

The last caller sounded as though he had a bad cold. "I know exactly who's behind this scam," he said, "and I intend to stop him. You can count on me. The public will be so grateful to me and my brothers for catching this ruthless young criminal that they'll grant us a lifelong pardon. Trust me. Just a few more hours and we'll have the little crook."

"Well, I guess there's a prank caller in every crowd," the announcer said. "Sorry about that, folks, but that's all the time we've got. Tune in tomorrow for our next phone-in show."

I yanked the hat off my head. That was no prank caller. I'd recognize that voice anywhere, even when he tried to disguise it. It was Eddy Banks! He really was planning to turn me in, in exchange for his own freedom. I had to get the aunties off the air before they got the Banks Brothers out of jail and me into it. The situation called for immediate action.

I remembered the aunties' note.

"Mom?" I called, dashing down the stairs.

"In the kitchen," she called back, "making us a lovely-old fashioned Sunday dinner."

I raced into the kitchen. "You said you found something stuck in the VCR slot. Where did you put it?"

"You mean that old picture of the aunties?"

"That's what was stuck in there?"

"Yes," she said. "I thought I told you."

"Where did you put it when you took it out of the VCR?"

"I don't know. Try the bookcase. Why did you put it in there, anyway? I still think that's what wrecked the TV."

I ran into the living room and found the old tintype photo on the bookcase. I took a good hard look at it. I realized that the couch in the old photo was the same one the aunties were sitting on on TV. What did it mean? And why had the photo been stuck in the VCR? It must be a clue — but I couldn't think what it meant. Who had put it in there, and why? Had the aunties put it there? Had they thought it would work like a video cassette? Was it possible that they'd got on TV by simply sticking a picture of themselves into the VCR and turning it on? If so, they weren't in a TV studio after all. They were inside the TV! They had never really left the house!

But if they'd got into the TV that way, maybe I could get them out. I glanced at my watch. Almost five p.m. My mom had a theatre group meeting at seven. The minute she left, I would put the aunties' picture back in the VCR and eject it back out. Maybe they'd come with it. I jumped around on the couch, feeling better than I had all weekend. When the Banks Brothers called, I'd tell them to go stick it in their ear.

"Jeremy, come for supper," Mom called.

"What are we having?" I asked. It smelled delicious.

She pulled a pan from the oven and set it triumphantly on the table. "Meatloaf, mashed potatoes, and carrots — a normal family meal for a change."

It wouldn't have been so bad if she hadn't let her artistic style get in the way. The meatloaf had been formed into the shape of a large dog standing in a snowdrift of mashed potatoes in a forest of carrot sticks.

"What's the matter?" she asked. "I thought you liked dogs."

"What kind of meat is it?" I asked suspiciously.

She grinned. "Beef. What did you think? Come on, eat up."

I carefully separated the trees from the snowdrift and chopped the ears and nose off the dog's head. It was okay.

My mother had to leave right after supper. I hurried back to the living room. My heart was thumping as I picked up the old metal photo of the aunties. I turned on the TV and waited for the fuzz to clear.

The aunties were discussing *me*.

"For his own protection," Mabel was saying, "I believe we should never mention his name."

"We already have mentioned his name," Gladys said.

"Yes, well, we cannot undo that. We can only hope that

no one heard us. Or that no one will put two and two together. From now on, we shall refer to him only as D. B., short for Dear Boy."

"But 'Boy' will narrow it to males and give a clue as to his age," Dotty protested.

"Nonsense," Gladys said. "Any male younger than ourselves is a boy. Besides, D. B. could stand for lots of things, like Dumb Bell or Ding Bat or Dull Brain or Dog's Breath or Doll Baby or Doodle Bug or Dust Bin or Dead Beat or Doggie Bag or Dumb Bunny or Dirt Bag or Dunce Bonnet or —"

Thanks a lot, I thought.

"So D. B. it is, girls, whenever we're talking about Jer — I mean D. B.," Dotty said. "But I'm sure he'll get our note and rescue us soon, so hadn't we better get on with our show while we still have time?"

"You bet!" Gladys said. "I'll be the host and you are my guests." She turned and looked out of the screen. "Hello, all you lovely people out there in TV land! In the absence of regular programming, we bring you live from right here inside the TV the first-ever true fake episode of the popular talk and game show 'Rrrrrrrrrrrrreal Women/Ideal Women'!" She clapped her gloves together madly. "Hey, come on, girls, help me clap." Mabel and Dotty clapped too. "Put 'em together, make some noise!" Gladys commanded. "Bang your purse, stomp your cane — they always make lots of noise whenever the host leaves a pause.

Hey, Mabel," she added, "what if you're wrong? What if you only *think* we're on TV and all this time we're really not?"

"I do not see where else we *could* be," Mabel replied slowly. "I suppose I could be wrong, but I so seldom am ... I really do not know ..."

"Oh, what does it matter?" Dotty cried. "Let's assume we are. I've dreamed of an audience all my life. And even if we're not on the air, we have to entertain ourselves somehow or we'll die of boredom."

"Right," Gladys said. "And the theme of our show tonight is: Gentlemen We Have Loved and Left."

I caught my breath. Were they planning to discuss me?

"Let's start with Dotty," Gladys went on. "Why did you never marry? You had plenty of beaux, as I recall."

"Oh yes." Dotty smiled. "Dozens. And I remember all their names. There were Harold and Charles from the felt factory, and Floyd, the boy next door. And Albert and John J. Templeman and Archie and Gilbert from school. And there was H. F. Noseworthy, the plumber, and William — there were two or three Williams — and Clarence, the billiards player, and Bertie and Ralph and Louis from the cycling club. Then there was Fritzie Uffelman, who took me out in his boat and we nearly capsized — do you remember? And Walter and Chadwick and their penpal Arthur, from the United States. Such a ladies' man. Morgan played the coronet in the marching band, and Clayton

I met at church, and Gerald and his cousin Freddie at a neighbourhood picnic. And there was Norman the bank clerk, and Ernest the bank manager, and Vernon with the fancy moustache. There were so many I simply couldn't choose. I was awfully fond of them all. My, I had a good time."

"Tell us about the men in *your* life, Mabel," Gladys said.

"No, don't," I said. "Cut the mushy stuff and get back here where you belong. We interrupt this program to bring you — back home!" I carefully placed the aunties' photo in the VCR slot. I put my finger on the EJECT button and pressed it. The aunties' photo popped back out of the slot. But the aunties stayed on TV.

"Ooh!" Dotty said. "I just felt a tingling sensation, didn't you, girls?"

"A tingling sensation?" Gladys asked. "Maybe your corset's too tight."

"I'm not wearing a corset, dear," Dotty said. "They're out of style, don't you know? Anyway, I don't feel tingly any more. It was just for a moment. I thought it was that same feeling we experienced when we set off on this trip."

I shoved the photo into the slot again.

"Ooh — there it is again!" Dotty squealed.

"I believe I feel something too," Mabel said. "Do you suppose D. B. is fiddling about with the video machine?"

"Perhaps he's trying to rescue us," Dotty cried. "Oh, I

knew we could count on him!"

"Not so fast," Gladys said. "If we're feeling tingly, we are probably getting electrified. He's not bringing us back, he's sending us farther along the way."

I stared at the screen, wondering what Gladys meant. I pressed REWIND, then STOP. It did seem as though the aunties had shrunk a little. They were not as close up as they had been. Or was it just my imagination? If I left their photo on rewind for a long time, would they get smaller and smaller until they disappeared? It was one way of getting them off TV. But where would they end up? I tried fast forward for a few seconds. It gave me a close-up of the aunties. They got larger and larger, until their faces filled the screen, until I was staring at an enormous stuffed nose. I didn't want to vaporize them! I quickly pressed REWIND, and then EJECT again, and popped the photo out of the machine.

"Okay," Gladys said. "I felt it that time too. What do you suppose is going on?"

I knew I was on to something. There was obviously some connection between the old photo and the aunties being on TV. But if ejecting the photo couldn't get the aunties back into the living room, what could?

For the next hour and a half the aunties rattled on about self-esteem.

"Yes, ladies and gentlemen," Gladys said, "self-esteem means that we esteem ourselves, or in other words, we think we're pretty great. I know I do. I have *loads* of self-esteem. Buckets, heaps, and piles of it. I think I'm awfully nice, don't you? Let's find out what our contestants have to say on the subject." She began clapping again. "Make some sound effects," she hissed at Mabel and Dotty. "Applause!"

"It would not be proper to clap for ourselves," Mabel said.

"Bang your cane, then," Gladys said.

"That would be undignified," Mabel replied.

"Fine," said Gladys, "do without clapping. See if I care."

"Now *you* are being undignified, Gladys," Dotty pointed out.

"Talk-show hosts aren't supposed to be dignified. And quit changing the subject," Gladys said. "We were talking about self-esteem."

"How on earth did you come up with such a topic?" Dotty asked.

"I saw it on D. B.'s report card," Gladys said. "'Low self-esteem.' I didn't know they studied that at school. I think he should have got a higher mark in it. He's got far too much self-esteem, if you ask me."

"I think it is a very silly expression," Mabel said. "I never heard it used in our day. When I was a girl, esteem was something you gave others, not yourself. Anyone who 'esteemed' himself would have been called a pompous humbug or a self-satisfied windbag. I am afraid I am suspicious of people who esteem themselves."

"But what does self-esteem have to do with either real or ideal women?" Gladys asked. "Does it have anything to do with why you never married? That might interest our audience. You first, Mabel."

"I do not generally discuss my personal life with strangers," Mabel said.

"I'm not a stranger," Gladys said. "I'm Gladys. I'm only pretending to be a talk-show host."

Dotty interrupted the argument by bursting into a song about meeting in the sweet by-and-by. I racked my brain wondering what to do next.

At last Dotty finished her song and sighed deeply.

"Oh dear, it's tiring being entertaining hour after hour. Life was so quiet back at D. B.'s. And yet I would rather be back with our dear young friend than here in this lonely place. Oh dear, where is my handkerchief?"

I looked around for a box of Kleenex.

"Oh, I *wish* we were back with D. B.," Dotty cried.

I heard a car screech to a halt in the driveway. The back door slammed as someone burst into the house.

Chapter Eleven

PHOTOGENIUS

MY MOM STORMED into the living room, angry and out of breath.

"Short meeting," I said, quickly flicking off the TV. I was relieved it was Mom and not someone more dangerous. "How did it go —"

"Turn on the TV, quickly! " she interrupted. "You won't *believe* what's happened."

"Uh — it's broken, remember?" I stammered.

"No, no, it's not." She crossed the room and turned it on. "It was all a mistake. We only *thought* it was broken." As soon as the aunties appeared, she pointed at them and cried, "Look! It's the aunties! Mabel, Gladys, and Dotty! On TV!"

"Incredible," I whispered. "How did you find out?"

"The whole town's talking about it! Everyone at the theatre meeting knew about it! I was the only one who didn't! We didn't even have a meeting. Everyone was so busy discussing the strange TV takeover. They're on every channel. People were teasing me that they look a lot like those dolls I made for the party, except they were convinced the women on TV were real, not dolls."

"Wh-what did you say?" I asked.

"I denied knowing anything about it, of course. I decided to make no comment until I'd checked into this further. I'm very upset. You were right all along, Jeremy — someone *did* kidnap the aunties. I thought you had them over at Rick's or something."

"No, I —"

"And whoever stole the aunties *also* stole my idea of putting microphones in them and making them appear to talk. That's what makes me really mad!"

I sighed in relief. Mom still didn't realize that the aunties were able to talk all by themselves. She had missed the point completely. Mothers get things so wrong.

"We'll call the cops and get them on the case," she said. "We'll find the thieves and sue them black and blue."

"Wait! Wait a minute!" I said. "We can't involve the police."

"You sound as if you know more about this mystery than you're telling me, Jeremy. Did you know they were on TV?"

"I had nothing to do with it. Honestly."

"Why do I have the feeling you're holding something back, son?"

"Well —" I began. "Well —"

"Well what?"

"Well, I don't know what's going on, but I'd really like to figure it out and get the aunties back here before anyone finds out for sure we're involved. There could be lawsuits and everything, because of lost air time, and we could be in a lot of trouble once everyone knows the aunties are ours."

"But we've done nothing wrong," my mother replied. "Whoever stole our aunties is responsible. Why shouldn't we get the police to catch them?"

"The police are probably on the case already," I said with a shiver. "I'm surprised they haven't traced them to us yet."

My mother thought over what I had said. In the silence we heard Gladys's voice on the TV.

"If I were going to change something in the world," she was saying, "I would make school optional. Only people who wanted to learn would be there. Anyone could go at any age — three or ninety-three. You could study whatever you wanted, and there would be no marks given and no attendance taken. No one would care if you were there or not, or learning or not."

Great idea! I'd vote for Gladys.

"Youngsters always get the short end of the stick," she went on. "For instance, when parents get divorced, the children get shuffled back and forth from one house to the other. I say the children should get the house for themselves, and the parents could travel back and forth for visits."

"An excellent proposal," Mabel agreed. "Now your turn, Dotty. What would you change?"

"She called her 'Dotty'!" Mom cried. "Did you hear? How would anybody know their *names*? Shh, listen."

"Can it be anything?" Dotty asked. "Anything at all?"

"Go for it," Gladys said. "Let your imagination run wild."

"Well," Dotty said, "if I could change anything in the world, I would change the three of us back into our former selves."

"What?" my mother asked.

"And we could go back to the good old days," Mabel said.

"Not exactly," Dotty said. "I've become rather fond of the modern world. I *like* automobiles and televisions, and even VCRs. What I would like is to be able to travel back and forth between past and present whenever we wished."

"Who's writing their script?" my mother asked. "I hate to admit it, but someone is doing a very convincing job. I can almost believe they're talking. If I didn't know better, I'd think they were real! It's not fair. They were *my* idea, not some doll thief's! I really think we should —"

"Get some sleep?" I finished for her. "You look tired, Mom. And I can hardly keep my eyes open. Why don't we talk about it tomorrow?" She was getting far too suspicious.

She glanced at her watch. "Hmm, almost ten. But there's something very strange going on, and I intend to get to the bottom of it."

Almost ten? The Banks Brothers' deadline was up!

The minute my mom went upstairs, I took the phone off the hook, so neither the Banks Brothers nor the police could call. Then I got busy. It seemed clear that the aunties had got on TV by sticking their photo in the VCR. If I was going to get them back, maybe all I needed to do was go in after them — the same way. My school photo was propped on a bookshelf, still unframed. It was a five-by-seven-inch close-up of my head and shoulders. I blew the dust off it, and was just about to shove it into the VCR when a sudden realization struck me. If my plan worked, I would appear on TV with the aunties, and anyone who knew me would instantly recognize me. I needed to disguise myself! I quickly got some glue and scissors and an old magazine. I found a page in the magazine that had a lot of black on it, and cut out a moustache, which I carefully glued onto my picture. It helped, but it wasn't enough. I cut out a wide black strip and poked two holes in it and glued the mask to the photo too, making sure the holes were positioned over my glasses. I cut out a little black triangle and glued it to my chin. Finally I added two black strips to the side of my face. I looked my picture over with satisfaction. Boy, would the aunties be surprised when a handsome pirate with beard, moustache, and sideburns suddenly appeared. I looked wicked, and very brave and confident.

I stuck my photo into the VCR, turned on the TV, and was just about to press PLAY when I had another thought that made me pause. My picture showed only my head and shoulders. What if my head and shoulders got sucked into the TV and the rest of my body was left behind? My mother would find it on the floor when she came down in the morning. She'd be terrified. I snatched my photo out of the slot and put it back on the shelf. It was obvious I needed a picture of my complete body. Thank goodness I'd thought of it in time.

I got out the photo albums and paged through them. There were lots of pictures of me, including full-length ones. But in most of them I was only two or five or seven years old. I opened a more up-to-date album. There I was — a little older — with Mom. Her arm was around my shoulder, and my arm was around her waist. If I cut very carefully, I could cut her out of the picture so she wouldn't zap into the TV with me. But then I would be missing my right arm, which I kind of needed. Anyway, the picture was over a year old. I didn't want to take this kind of journey knowing less than I did now. I turned the pages, but there were no more pictures. I had broken the camera last Christmas, trying to get the film out. Where could I get an up-to-date photo? Of course I couldn't let anybody else take my picture, or the person would recognize me once I got on TV. The mall downtown had one of those little photo booths where you can take your own picture, but it wouldn't take a full-length view. Besides, the mall would be closed by now. If only I had a Polaroid camera. Wait a minute — Rick had a Polaroid! Unfortunately, it was too late to bike over to his place. In fact I was feeling too tired to think straight. I dragged myself up to bed. My plan would have to wait till tomorrow.

✧

First thing next morning I biked to Rick's place. I could hear Solange barking, but no one answered the bell. Rick and I knew where each other's spare house keys were hidden. His was in a magnetic box behind the drainspout. I let myself in. Solange had a fit, barking and jumping all over me. I didn't know if she was happy to see me or trying to be a guard dog. I found Rick's camera in his room. I had assumed it would have a timer so I could set it to take my own picture, but it didn't seem to have. Holding it as far away as my arms would stretch, I pushed the button. Out slid a picture. As the image gradually became visible, I could see that all I had was an out-of-focus photo of my head. Oh, this was never going to work. How could I get a full-length photo? I sat on the edge of Rick's bed, completely out of ideas.

Solange was still barking at me. She stood at the bedroom door, looking as though she wanted something. In the hope of shutting her up, I followed her into the kitchen. Her food and water bowls were full. She jumped up at the cupboard.

"What do you want?" I asked. "What are you trying to

tell me?" Then I realized. She was trying to reach the toaster!

"Okay," I said. "I'll make you some toast if you quit barking before the neighbours call the police. Deal?" I found some bread and put a slice in the toaster. It felt kind of weird being alone in Rick's house — making toast for a dog.

The toast popped up — and a thought popped into my head. Rick was always bragging about how smart poodles were. Was a poodle smart enough to take a Polaroid picture? I carried the toast into the bedroom, Solange yapping at my heels.

"Be patient," I said. "You'll get it in a minute." I propped up the camera on Rick's chest of drawers and sighted through the viewfinder. Then I lifted Solange onto the chest of drawers and demonstrated how I could press the shutter button with my nose. She tried to bite my nose. I gave her a bit of the toast to calm her down. She snapped at my nose again, looking expectant.

"No, that's not the trick. You're supposed to put *your* nose on the camera, like this, and then you'll get more toast, okay?"

She gave the camera a quick sniff, then sat up and begged.

"I thought Rick said you were smart," I said. "Well, now's the time to prove it. Press the button with your *nose* — like this — and you'll get some toast. Like this — see?" I popped a chunk of toast in my mouth. "Mmm! Yum! Delicious. I'm going to do it again. Would you like some?

Just press the button with your nose, and —"

It worked! Solange pressed her nose down on the button, there was a noise, and a picture slid out. Solange whimpered and jumped to the floor.

"Yes! Way to go! Good girl!" I jumped up and down in excitement. "Here's your toast. Good girl!" I gave her the last big chunk. "Wow, you are smart. Can you do it again?" I watched the photo develop while I made another slice of toast in the kitchen. Solange had taken a pretty good picture of the head of Rick's bed and a poster on the wall.

"Atta girl!" I said. "Let's do it again." I led Solange back to the bedroom, tossing the hot toast from hand to hand, and set her back on the chest of drawers behind the camera. Quickly I backed over to the bed. She pressed the button before I got into position, but I gave her some toast anyway. The photo, when it developed, showed most of me. We were getting there. But there were only two pictures left on the film. Before I could get into position Solange pressed the button again.

"Okay, okay, take it easy. Yes, you're doing the right thing, just not so fast — there's only one left." I tossed her a chunk of toast, which she caught, and while she gobbled it I stood in what I hoped was the right spot. Solange pressed the button and I tossed her the rest of the toast.

"Good doggie. Let's hope this worked," I said. "You know, maybe I could change my mind about poodles." As I waited for the last photo to develop, I heard a key turn in the lock.

There was no time to hide under the bed or in the closet. Solange skittered out the door, yapping. I shoved the photos inside my shirt and peeked into the hall.

"Ah, Jeremy!" Professor Ricketts exclaimed. "You came over to play with Solange while Rick's away. What a thoughtful boy. Isn't he a good friend, Solange? Isn't he good to come and keep you company while Papa's at work? You even made her some toast — I can smell it. Jeremy, I hope your mother appreciates what a considerate son she has. Rick never thinks of things to do for others. It never crosses his mind."

"I know," I said. "He was supposed to phone me from Calgary and he hasn't called once."

"Oh, he did try," Professor Ricketts assured me. "He called me late last night and said your phone had been busy for hours."

I was dying to see how the last photo had turned out. "I've got to get going," I said. "Goodbye, Solange. Goodbye, Professor Ricketts."

"Come back and play with Solange any time," he said. "She's really missing Rick."

I had a brilliant idea. "Could I babysit her for a day or two till Rick gets back?" I asked. "We could keep each other company."

"She'd love that," he said. "I'll pack her things. She's

got an appointment at the beauty parlour tomorrow, and at the vet's on Wednesday. Don't forget. I'll write down the times." He got Solange's things — two large bagfuls — and thanked me again for my thoughtfulness.

"Thank *you*," I said. "She's a fantastic dog."

I biked home as fast as I could. Solange sat in the carrier, her ears blowing in the breeze. If I could get my mom used to the advantages of having such a clever and useful dog around the house, she might break down and let me get my own. We ran inside and I dumped the photos out of my shirt onto the kitchen table. Yes! There was a perfect full-length picture of me! Not a toe or a hand or a bit of hair missing. Solange had done it! My luck must be turning around. I made myself a leftover-meatloaf sandwich and opened a can of ginger ale. I was just about to draw a disguise on my picture with felt pens, when I had a thought. I brought the aunties' old tintype out to the kitchen and examined it closely. On TV the aunties were wearing the clothes I had last seen them in — plus the goggles and leather helmets — *not* the clothes in the tintype. What did that mean? It must mean that what you were wearing at the time you got zapped was what you appeared in on TV. So maybe I didn't need a disguised photo after all. What I *needed* to do was disguise *myself*! How about a sheet draped completely over me, with two eyeholes cut out like a Hallowe'en ghost's? No — too awkward to move around in. There had to be a better idea. I thought and thought, and at last it came to me. It was so simple, and in a way so obvious, yet so perfect! But did I really want to embarrass myself like that? Yes, I told myself firmly. I would do whatever it took to get the aunties off the air. My freedom depended on it. If I didn't get them off the TV, I would end up in jail — or at least, in a home for young offenders. Solange followed me around the house from room to room as I collected bits and pieces for my costume.

I took Solange out for a bathroom break before my mom got home, then made her a nice bed out of bath towels in my closet. I put some food in there for her and hoped she wouldn't bark. There was no need for Mom to know right away that she was visiting. I would keep Solange in my room for awhile to prove to Mom that she hadn't even known a dog was in the house. Solange gave a little yip during supper, but Mom didn't seem to hear it. I checked her a couple of times during the evening, but she seemed to like her new doghouse.

I was waiting for my mom to go up to bed, when I had a sudden thought that made me weak: what if I got into the TV with the aunties and couldn't get back out? I could be trapped in there with them for ever! Why hadn't I thought of that before? My plan was obviously incomplete — I had a pretty good idea how to get into the TV, but no idea how to get out. Which was worse, I wondered: to be trapped on TV for life or trapped in jail for life? But if there was a way into the TV, there had to be a way out. It was just that the aunties hadn't thought of it. Being much smarter than they were, I would soon figure it out. Maybe if I knew more about TVs ... I spotted the library books on the coffee table — the ones about TV that I had brought the aunties the day they disappeared. The top one was called *How Television Really Works.* I gathered up the books, said good night to Mom, and went up to my room to study and plan.

Solange joined me in bed, and by the light of my Mickey Mouse flashlight we examined the pictures in the books — little diagrams showing how our eyes see a figure upside-down and how a camera lens works the same way. I learned what makes a light-bulb light up and how TV microwaves are bounced from transmitters to satellites and cables. It was all pretty boring. I tried to take more of an interest. I had to take an interest — my life as a free boy depended on it. But I found myself reading the same paragraph over and over ... I think I dozed off for a while. I woke up with a jump, having had a strange mini-dream about taking the TV apart with the screwdriver and finding the aunties inside, all small and shrunken, like little rag-dolls. They weren't very happy about being rescued, and yelled at me in tiny, fuzzy voices. But I thought they were much better small. More manageable.

I started thinking I must be totally nuts to believe the aunties could have got themselves through the VCR and into the TV. They'd never fit. It was a ridiculous idea. Yet they were in there somewhere, and I was in a mess. It amazed me how they could get me into trouble even when they weren't here. And it was *big* trouble this time. I was in way over my head. Where was Rick when I needed him? He'd been gone two days — it seemed much longer — and I was in this totally alone. Except for Solange. At least I had someone to share my worries and comfort me with a warm wet tongue.

I went back to the books. I learned that a scientist named Dr. V. K. Zworykin developed the first TV receiver in the 1920s, but that almost no one had one at home until the 1950s. I learned that since electromagnetic waves travel in straight lines, they can travel only 240 kilometres before the earth curves too much. I learned that a communications satellite 35,900 kilometres up in space moves along with the earth as it orbits and can cover one-third of the earth day and night. The TVs in our houses act as receivers that pick up microwaves and convert them into pictures. All this information seemed pretty far-fetched. I got sleepier and sleepier. I picked up the last book, and tiredly started reading rows of numbers that looked like scientific formulas. It took me a minute to realize that this wasn't a library book, but the old photographer's diary. It must have been lying open on the coffee table underneath the other books. On the facing page was handwriting I recognized. It was Mabel's writing — and it was addressed to me.

Chapter Twelve

THE INSIDE-OUT MAN

IT WAS THE AUNTIES' note! It was written as a poem, and called:

Goodbye, Dear Boy

Dear boy, upon the eve of our departure
We pause to write a note of sad farewell,
We'll always fondly cherish your dear memory
For if we'll meet again, no one can tell.

We never chose to be your long-term houseguests,
And certainly we had no invitation;
The three of us arrived upon your sofa
By strange photography miscalculation.

We found ourselves in something of a pickle,
It truly was embarrassing and shocking,
We knew we shouldn't stay, yet couldn't leave you,
Trapped helplessly in bodies of stuffed stocking.

Our hosts — that's you and your dear mother —
Did what you could to make our visit pleasant.
But it was quite a shock for us three ladies,
Zapped rudely from the past into the present.

At first, our eccentricities amused you
(The sentiment was mutual, never doubt),

But time soon changes interest to annoyance
And even stuffed guests wear their welcome out.

And so we reached at last the sad conclusion
The time had come to go our separate ways;
There had to be some clever way of leaving,
But how? The question bothered us for days.

Since we arrived by photo-television
We thought that this same magic combination
Would prove to be the obvious way of leaving
By some unknown reversing transportation.

And then, dear boy, you bought a new contraption —
A VCR, that hooks up with TV!
We really think that it is just the ticket,
To get us home — we all must wait and see.

With careful thought and planning we've decided
(It's best for you and us, we strongly feel)
To leave the stuffy modern world of dollhood
And go back to the days when we were real.

We've had some laughs, dear boy, we'll truly miss you;
We hope you know it's been a hard decision.
And if we could, we'd surely take you with us
Into the past — by way of television.

And so, with thanks, regret, and yet excitement,
We see no reason now for a delay,
We'll stick our photo in the VCR slot
And press the little button that says PLAY.

So the note had been there on the coffee table all the time. I must have laid the library books on top of it without seeing it. It seemed appropriate, somehow, that the aunties had written it in the photographer's diary. It was sort of the next chapter of their unusual life. Reading the poem made me miss them so much that I nearly ran down and turned on the TV just so I could see and hear them again. Had I really made them feel so unwelcome that they wanted to leave? That gave me a bad feeling. I hadn't meant to. I liked them — they were my friends. I would do anything to get them back!

Their note did prove, anyway, that they had got on TV by sticking their photo in the VCR slot, just as I had guessed. Those aunties — thinking they could get back to the past through the TV! They had the most ridiculous ideas sometimes. But I still had no clue how to get them out without getting myself trapped in there with them. It made me tired thinking and thinking about it, not knowing what to do. I cuddled up against Solange, and went to sleep.

Next morning, I hid Solange in the closet and went downstairs. I found Mom outside, searching the front flowerbed.

"Mom?" I asked. "What are you doing?"

"Checking for clues," she replied. "The person or persons who broke in and stole the aunties might have left a footprint or something." She came back in a few minutes, looking disappointed. "Of course, an entire *team* of kidnappers could have come in through the garage without us noticing anything out of place. It's such a mess. We should take the entire contents to the dump. We'd never miss anything, and I'd have a nice dry place to park the convertible. I wouldn't have to bail it out every time it rains." She sighed. "I think I asked you to clean the garage up. That can be your job for today while I'm gone. Maybe you'll find my radio hat." She kissed the top of my head and went off to work.

But I had much more urgent things to do than clean the garage. Her comment about the dump had given me a good idea. I put on the radio hat, fed Solange, set her in my bike carrier, and headed straight for the dump. I needed something more than just books to teach me about TV.

I had never been to the dump before, but I knew where it was, on the edge of the city. I biked for a long time. Finally I saw a sign: LANDFILL SITE. A long chain-link fence and a padlocked gate made it look as though the dump-keepers were worried someone might break in. I couldn't even see any garbage, just a parking lot and some huge bins beyond the fence. A small building with two doors stood next to the gate. I knocked on one of the doors. It was opened by a tall, thin man with grey-brown hair. He was wearing a grey-brown uniform with two badges on it. One said "Earl." The other said "Sanitation Engineer."

"Hello," I said. "Can you let me into the dump, please? I'm looking for something."

"Sorry. City property. No trespassing." His voice sounded vague and he looked out into space when he talked.

"I won't disturb anything," I said. "I'll just take a quick look around and be gone in fifteen minutes, okay?"

"Sorry, we don't do tours except in the spring."

"What are you afraid of?" I asked. "That I might steal some garbage? All I want is an old TV to take apart."

"Sorry. We don't accept TVs or other large electrical appliances, except on three Saturdays a year. You'll find them marked on the municipal calendar."

"Are you real?" I asked. "Or some kind of robot?" I don't usually talk to adults that way, but I was exhausted from the long bike ride and exasperated at not getting in.

"Sorry," Earl said. "We don't have robots here due to government cutbacks."

I shook my head and turned my bike around.

"Are you really looking for an old TV?" he asked suddenly, in a more interested voice. I nodded. "I may be able to help you. Just a minute, while I change."

Earl seemed like a very odd guy. He soon seemed even odder. He stepped back inside the building and began peeling off his coverall. He turned it inside out, put it back on again, and came out through the other door with a smile. His uniform was now blue. It had two badges on it. One said "Earl." The other said, "Used Equipment."

"So," he said, in a cheery voice, "looking for a TV, are you? Step right this way."

I stepped inside the second door, into a room filled with all kinds of appliances.

"Here's a nice one," Earl said. "Good as new. Fifty bucks and it's yours."

Fifty bucks? I felt in my pockets. Counting all my change, I had about three dollars.

"Don't you have anything cheaper?" I asked. "I just want an old one to take apart. I don't care if it works."

"You want to buy a broken TV?" Earl shook his head. "Some people sure are strange."

He disappeared into the back of the shop and returned with a battered TV. The glass was cracked, as though someone had thrown something at it because they didn't like the show that was on.

"Three bucks and it's yours." I handed over the money. "How about a remote control to go with it?"

"No, I don't need a remote control," I said. "I've already got one, thanks."

"Got a car?" he asked.

I shook my head. "I'm way too young to drive."

"So how do you plan to get the TV home?"

I hadn't thought of that.

"I've got a good deal for you," he said. "I'll sell you that baby carriage in the corner — only ten bucks, real cheap."

I looked to where he was pointing. An old-fashioned, pale blue baby buggy with rusty springs was parked in the corner.

"But I haven't got ten bucks," I said, my shoulders slumping.

"Then I'll make you an even better deal," he said. "I'll trade you the carriage for your hat."

"Oh, no, I can't sell the hat! It's not mine!" I reached up and put my hands firmly on my mother's radio hat.

"All right, how about your dog, then? My baby carriage for your dog. Fair trade."

"No! The dog's not mine either!"

"You seem to be in possession of a lot of things that aren't yours," Earl said. "You can get in trouble for that kind of thing, you know."

I sighed. "I guess I can't take the TV after all."

"Sorry, you bought it, it's yours. How you get it home is not my business."

It was turning into a lousy day. As I turned to leave, the phone rang.

"City landfill site," Earl said. "Yes, inspector, sir. Inspection, sir? Today, sir? Yes, sir. Right away, sir." He peeled off his coverall and quickly began turning it inside-out. "Store's closing, kid, you're going to have to get out of here. Goodbye. You didn't see anything."

"But you owe me three bucks," I said.

"I'm in a hurry," he said. "Move it out, I've got to lock

this place."

I leaned against the door. "I'm not moving until I get my money back."

He glared at me. "Okay, take the TV, and take the baby carriage too! Just get out of here, okay?" He threw the TV in the buggy, and held the door as I wheeled it outside. He put the uniform back on and became a grey-brown sanitation engineer once again, complete with vacant stare.

"Thanks for giving me the buggy for free," I said.

"Don't mention it," he said.

"Why not?" I asked.

"Why not what?"

"Why not mention it?"

"'Don't mention it' is another way of saying, 'think nothing of it.'"

"Of what?" I asked.

"Of what I did."

"What did you do?" I asked.

"I gave you something for free."

"Yes, that's great. Thanks a lot."

"Don't mention it."

"I *didn't* and I *won't*. What's the big secret?" I wondered if there was more to Earl than met the eye.

"You're a trouble-maker, I can see that," he said, glaring into space. "I've got your number."

"How could you?" I asked. "You don't even know my

name." All I needed was another weirdo like Eddy Banks having my number and making threatening phone calls.

"Just beat it, okay?" he said, through gritted teeth.

I gave up. With a guy like that you could spend hours arguing and never get anywhere. My mom says it's the unusual people who make life interesting.

It was a bit of a challenge pushing the buggy in front of my bike. First I tried to steer with one hand on my handlebar and the other on the buggy handle. I zigzagged along the shoulder of the road, the buggy creaking and squeaking. I fell off twice. Solange leaped out of the carrier and onto the hood of the buggy, where I had a hard time seeing past her. Then I tried two hands on the buggy handle while steering my bike with my knees. It was in this awkward position that I finally reached the downtown area. On the street by the C-KIT TV studio, the weirdest sight I've ever seen met my eyes.

The city had gone totally wild! The street was crowded with people marching and carrying signs, and there was a big shouting match going on between two groups near the television building. I edged my bike a little closer. The larger group was shouting angrily, "TV is our right! We're prepared to fight, fight, fight!" The signs they were carrying said, "You'll Pay For This!.," "Give Us Back Our Shows," "Greyout Victims Unite," "Something's Got to Be Done — This Is an Outrage," and "Anti-Aunties!"

The other group was smaller and quieter, and seemed

much happier. They were chanting, "Up with the Aunties, Rah Rah Rah! Down with TV, Ha Ha Ha!" Their signs said things such as "Grey Power," "Long Live The Aunties," "Air Pirates Forever" and "Pro-Auntie!" Most of the members of the smaller group were wearing odd clothes — big flowery hats, long dresses, and gloves. It took me a minute to realize that they were supposed to look like aunties. Even the men. It sure looked weird to see aunties with beards.

A couple of cops were trying to keep order. One of them was the red-haired Constable Heaves. I quickly ducked out of his line of vision. In fact, I thought it might be a good idea to get out of there altogether. It felt dangerous to be in the middle of all these people who felt so strongly about the aunties. Up until now I had been almost the only one who knew of their existence. Now it seemed they were public property. And some people actually *liked* them taking over the TV? That was a surprise.

I continued towards home. About halfway there, the front buggy wheels locked. By tipping the buggy up with the front wheels in the air, I managed to keep it rolling along. My back ached like crazy. I saw four TVs out at the ends of driveways, one of them very near my place. I guess the owners didn't realize the dump wouldn't pick them up with the other garbage. I could have taken them for free! I also saw about five people dressed like aunties. Were they real old ladies, or just people dressed up to look that way? Was I going crazy?

When I finally got home, I crammed the buggy into the garage and carried the TV into the living room. I was starving by then, not having had any lunch, so I made myself a plate of orange-and-lime Jell-O sandwiches. (Jell-O sandwiches are my favourite, and very fast to make. First you spread margarine on four or five slices of bread — I prefer white. Then you sprinkle Jell-O powder onto the margarine and put another slice of bread on top, and so on, in alternating colours. It looks great and tastes even better. It's a recipe I made up one day when we were out of peanut butter and mayo.)

After lunch I found a screwdriver and took the back off the television I'd bought. I was determined to figure out how to safely rescue those troublemaking aunties of mine. There was definitely no room for three aunties in there, even small ones. The space was filled with a big bulb-like thing wrapped in copper wires, two silver boxes labelled VHF and UHF, a whole bunch of plastic-coated wires — red, yellow, blue, green, brown — and a really cool circuit board. The circuit board was on the bottom. It was covered in a sort of code, with little coloured beads or bumps with mysterious labels, such as L202, TP-13, R174, and about a hundred other numbers. On the side of this board it said, "Fail Safe Board," "Sync Circuit," "Error Amp," "Horiz Drive," "Colour Killer," "High Fly-Back Transformer." It was all very mysterious. I was about to twist off some of the copper wires when I saw a little warning notice that said, "Caution. Yoke is permanently bonded to picture tube. Do not attempt to separate." There were a couple of other little notices hidden away in places where they were hard to see: "Warning! This picture tube employs integral implosion." "Caution: hi-vac picture tube. Dangerous to handle. Refer servicing to qualified personnel only." "To avoid possible exposure to X-radiation, take protective measures." It was kind of scary. What if I touched the wrong thing and nuked myself? My mother would come home and find no sign of me except a mysterious burned-out box sitting on a black hole in the carpet. I couldn't do that to her. I had to stay alive to rescue the aunties. If I didn't, there was no one else to do it.

I put down the screwdriver and switched on the TV — not the broken one — to see what the aunties were up to.

"Perhaps we should resign ourselves to the fact that we are going to be stuck here for ever," Gladys was saying. "And I mean for ever. For the rest of our unnatural lives."

"Oh, say it's not so!" Dotty put her glove to her heart. "That is a fate worse than death. I'm afraid I shall become hysterical."

"Enough nonsense," Mabel said firmly. "We must never give in to despair. I am confident that D. B. will rescue us. Either sooner or later."

"I bet he doesn't even miss us," Gladys said. "I have to admit, we weren't exactly nice to him the last few days."

"Nonsense," Mabel said. "We were perfectly polite at

all times. We must have patience. He is an intelligent and loyal friend. We are missing from the couch. He will try to find us. We must trust that that is true."

Great, I thought. I had the awful feeling that I was going to disappoint them. I would have been much happier if they hadn't trusted me. Having them depend on me was scary. Since when was a boy responsible for three grown-up women? It wasn't fair. It scared me that they seemed as worried as I was. I had wasted a whole day getting a TV to study, and I hadn't learned one useful thing. I wished Rick would call. He'd probably have an idea of what to do. That was when I suddenly remembered that I had taken the phone off the hook the night before. I put the receiver back in the cradle. The phone immediately rang.

Chapter Thirteen

PAST THE DEADLINE

"HELLO?" I SAID.

"Time's up, sonny," growled a familiar voice, "and we ain't got our money. You missed your deadline."

"I couldn't —" I began.

"You've broke your promise, sonny. And that's something a Banks can't forgive."

"I *tried* to send you the money," I said. "I called every courier company in the phone book and not one of them is open on Sunday."

"Ho," Eddy said. "A likely story. Think you can fool an experienced man of the world like me, do you?"

"I heard you on the radio phone-in," I said. "I know what you're trying to do. You're planning to turn me in so you'll be a hero and they'll let you and your brothers out of jail early!"

"So what if I am?" Eddy said. "Watcha gonna do about it, sonny boy? Report me for having prior knowledge of a crime? I'm already in jail, remember? You just send me that money, sonny. And I mean now."

"How do I know you won't report me as soon as you get it?"

"Don't you trust me?"

What could I say? Yes would be a lie, and no would make him mad. "I think I know how the aunties got on TV," I said. "I know there's got to be a way I can get them off."

"Never mind that," Eddy said. "I'm gonna give you the benefit of the doubt about the courier, but I'll tell you something. Us boys here in the pen are missing TV. It's one of the few pleasures left to us fellows who've had our human rights and freedoms stripped away from us by an uncaring society. It's one of our few small comforts in the long lonely days of our incarceration." He paused, and I could hear snuffling in the background. Then he cleared his throat and spoke gruffly. "Us boys in the big house don't like someone messing with our favourite shows. It makes us antsy. It's our right to watch TV and someone's taken that right away. If we don't get it back there's going to be a prison revolt! And guess who we'll blame? You! That's who. This is all your fault. You and those three old dames. Me and Mort and Harvey know it. I can't wait to turn you in. But first, you send me the VCR and the reward dough."

"If you're going to turn me in anyway, why should I send you the stuff?" I asked.

"Because if you don't" — Eddy spoke very slowly — "me and my brothers got friends on the outside who'd just as soon blow your little lights out as look at you. All's I need to do is give the word, and you're toast, sonny. Get me?"

"Wait — wait," I begged. "Just give me twenty-four more hours."

"Now you're talking. Thirty-six and it's a deal."

"Fifty," I said boldly.

"Forty-two, and not a minute less!" Eddy said.

"Okay," I said. "Today is Tuesday, three p.m. That gives me till Thursday at five-thirty p.m. Deal?"

"Deal," Eddy said. "Break that deadline, and you'll be a headline. You got till Thursday afternoon, and then — bye-bye." He hung up with a loud click.

I hung up, giggling. I had got the better of Eddy Banks. Instead of twenty-four hours, or even forty-two, he had given me *fifty and a half* hours! Ha ha, I sure fooled him. But I stopped laughing when I realized that if Eddy Banks couldn't count the hours in a day, he might easily call the cops, or his criminal pals, in forty hours — or even twenty. He had probably called them already, and was phoning just to tease me. Why would I trust a crook to keep his word? Maybe I should box up the VCR and the money and ship them to him right now. But that would be plain stupid. I needed the VCR more than ever now. It was my main link to the aunties. If I had any hope of getting them back it was through the video machine. Why had I been so dumb as to believe that giving the Banks Brothers the money and the VCR would buy them off? Eddy Banks was probably leaning against the prison phone laughing at me. I *had* to get the aunties off the air!

I turned on my radio hat to help me think. The local news was all about the parades and demonstrations downtown.

"Traffic had to be rerouted off the main street today because of crowds of protesters," the announcer said. "Police estimates put the number between three and five hundred, many of them dressed in the style of the three women who have been airjacking all the TV channels for the last three days. An eighty-one-year-old protester was injured when a sign carried by an anti-Auntie demonstrator fell on his head. He was taken to hospital where he was treated for minor injuries and released."

Wow — it was dangerous out there! I felt terrible — as if the injury were my fault. I had to do something before anyone else got hurt. The screen door banged. I whipped off my hat, thinking it was Mom, home early. But it was only the paper boy. I hid the TV I'd bought, and the radio hat, behind an armchair, and went to get the paper.

TV OR NOT TV? the headlines read.

No demands have yet been made by the persons responsible for the disruption of television viewing throughout the province. Three elderly women, or their associates, are holding the public hostage by taking over all television networks and affiliate stations. Investigators remain baffled about the case, although they admit that members of the PQE (Parents for Quality Entertainment) have been questioned. Police apparently also suspect that computer hackers working from the local university may be responsible, and that the TV blackout is a student experiment or prank that got out of hand. Networks are discussing offering a reward to get the pirate station off the air. Lawsuits are pending.

A grainy picture of the aunties on TV accompanied the article. I looked at it closely. You couldn't really tell it was Mabel, Gladys, and Dotty. It was hard to tell from the picture if they were dolls or slouchy people.

There was another article on page two.

WHO ARE THEY AND WHAT DO THEY WANT?

Who are the three women who call themselves Mabel, Gladys, and Dotty? Disgruntled viewers are helpless to do anything about the monopoly of their TVs by the three seniors. Members of the public are asked to contact local police if they have any information about the three women. So far no one has come forward. In a recent poll, eighty per cent of the viewing public expressed anger over the pre-empting of their TV shows. A smaller percentage lauded the elderly women who have had the courage to go up against the powerful national networks — and beat them at their own game. They have been compared to Greenpeace activists, The Raging Grannies, and other organizations fighting for minority rights. Although the women's demands have never been clearly outlined, they are, ironically, against television and criminals, seemingly unaware that they themselves are television criminals. Who are they and what do they want? No one seems to know.

How they got on the air is not the only mystery. What is equally mysterious is how they can survive for so long without food, drink, sleep, or exercise. Experts examining tapes of the broadcast believe the show is being filmed live. No splicing or breaks in the film are evident. If that is the case, can the aunties really stay awake twenty-four hours day after day without food or water? This may go down as the longest continual sit-in in history.

I read everything I could find about the aunties, including five angry letters to the editor. Even the fashion page mentioned the aunties, in an article entitled "Hats and Gloves Back in Style." Rose, from Rose's Clothes, was quoted as saying that she was sold out of aunties-style clothing. Business, she said, had never been so brisk.

When I looked at my watch it was nearly five. Soon Mom would be home. I took Solange for a quick walk, then settled her upstairs in my closet. I thought about finding a cookbook and making supper for Mom. She would be surprised. I yawned. I yawned again, and decided to lie down on the couch for just five minutes before starting supper. Another wasted day. Time was ticking away. Tick, tock, tick, tock. I closed my eyes and drifted away.

Even in my dreams I could hear a clock ticking. It was the clock on the wall of Earl's Used Equipment shop. I was trapped inside a garbage compactor, and Earl, who kept changing his uniform inside-out from brown to blue, was shoving a remote control in my face. "Buy a remote control," he insisted. "Control a remote buy. Rebuy a controlled moat. Recontrol by a moat!"

I felt a hand shake my shoulder.

"It's almost six. Did you fall asleep? Why didn't you start supper, or at least set the table?"

My eyes flew open. I was staring up at my mom's face.

"Welcome to a higher level of consciousness," she said. "I'll give you a few minutes to clear the fog while I skim the paper, and then let's eat. I'm hungry."

Being awake felt great. And I had just dreamed up a great — no, a *brilliant* — idea! Really, sometimes I get much better ideas when I'm sleeping than when I'm awake. I was going in after the aunties. The question had been how to do it without getting trapped in there myself. My dream had given me the answer. I could hardly wait to put my plan into action. I would have supper with Mom, play a game, whatever. The minute Mom was safely in bed, I would put on my disguise and zap myself to the rescue.

I was feeling so good, I went to the kitchen and set the table without being asked a second time. Mom joined me a few minutes later. "Look at this!" She pointed to a page of the newspaper. "There are three new babies in the births column today named Mabel — and a little Dotty too."

"You're kidding!" I laughed.

"Did you see the article about the reward?" She passed me the paper. It was on the first page, in a box outlined in red. I wondered how I had missed it. "Read it aloud while I nuke the soup," she said.

"INVESTIGATORS NARROW SEARCH TO CITY," I read.

Detectives working on the mysterious Air Pirates case, which has all but put an end to TV viewing across the province, say they are focussing their search on this area. A spokesman for the Auntie Task Force says an anonymous tip has led police to believe that the crime is being engineered from this very city. "It is only a matter of time before we narrow it down and apprehend the perpetrators," says Constable Rodney Heaves, assistant to the chief investigator. "We have some clues, and we will systematically track them down. This crime will not go unpunished."

Meanwhile, a reward of twenty thousand dollars — no questions asked — has been offered by television companies whose programs have been blacked out since the three elderly women took over the air-waves last Friday.

"Twenty thousand dollars!" Mom exclaimed, setting a bowl of tomato soup in front of me. "No questions asked! I think that's a point in our favour, don't you? If no questions are asked, no one will find out where we got our information."

"What information?" I asked.

"I'm really not sure I should tell you. It's only a suspicion at this point. I hesitate to even mention it."

"I think you'd better tell me whatever you know," I said nervously.

"Well, all right," she said. "It's only this. Which person knows the aunties exist, and has access to this house any time he wants?"

"Me?" I asked in a small, shocked voice. "You mean you'd actually turn me over to the cops? You'd trade me for twenty thousand dollars? That's like selling your own child, Mom." I could feel tears forming in the corners of my eyes, and blinked them away. "I can't believe you'd do that."

"Don't be silly, Jeremy. I mean Rick. Rick knows we made the aunties, and he has access to this house any time he wants."

"You think *Rick* put the aunties on TV? Oh no, he had nothing to do with it."

"Think about it, Jeremy," she said. "When did the aunties disappear? And when did Rick disappear? Is he really in Calgary? We both know he's good with computers. I wouldn't be one bit surprised if he took the aunties to his place and — made a video or something. He might be clever enough to get it on the air somehow."

"I was over at his place just yesterday," I said, "and

there was nothing suspicious going on."

"What were you doing at his place if he's not there?" Mom asked.

"Uh — just teaching his dog a trick," I said. "Take my word for it, Mom. I'm one hundred per cent sure Rick had nothing to do with this."

"I certainly *hope* he's not involved," she said. "He's like a second son to me. As I say, it's only a suspicion at this point. But you must admit there are a lot of coincidences ... Giving the police that many clues should be enough to get us the reward, don't you think? I believe I'll give them a call."

I couldn't finish my soup. I told Mom I had a stomach-ache, and went up to my room.

Chapter Fourteen

THE PERFECT DISGUISE

THERE COULD BE no more delays. I was going on my mission tonight. Solange nosed about expectanly, wondering why I was rushing around. I laid the pieces of my disguise out on the bed. My face was the problem. My glasses and freckles needed some camouflage. I went into the bathroom and found a little case of pink cheek powder, and brushed some on. It hid the freckles pretty well. My glasses were too identifiable — square, with bluish rims. My mom's round, wire-rimmed sunglasses were on the bathroom windowledge. If I could pop the lenses out of them and attach my lenses to them, they would make me look quite different.

Back in my own room I sat on the bed to do the lens switch. The sunglass lenses popped out easily. It was my own that were the problem. I almost broke one. It was difficult to see what I was doing without my glasses on, but I couldn't take them apart unless I took them off. I found some tape and carefully stuck my square lens in behind the round wire rim. It was tricky work. I squinted and focussed as hard as I could. It gave me a headache. The tape was invisible while I was working with it, but when I put the glasses on to check in the mirror, the tape was pretty obvious. I hoped it wouldn't show on TV.

There was a loud knock on my bedroom door. I quickly shoved the glasses under my pillow and the costume and Solange under the bed. I dived under the covers, being careful not to squash the pillow, and said sleepily, "Come in."

My mother marched into the room. "What is the meaning of *this*, young man?" she asked, whipping something out from behind her back.

"What?" I squinted blearily.

"Your school photo, that's what! What have you done to it?"

"Oh, uh, that." I could dimly make out some geometric black shapes. "Oh, nothing. Just having a little fun, that's all."

"A little fun! I paid good money for this photo and now you've ruined it. It's the only picture of you I've got from this whole year."

"Sorry," I said.

"Sorry! Is that all you've got to say? Jeremy, I would expect something like this from a four-year-old, but not a boy your age. Defacing your own photo, blocking off the eyes, adding a moustache and beard ... If you ask me, it's got deep psychological implications."

"It was just a joke," I murmured.

"Was it? I think it was a cry for help. This picture says

to me that half of you wants to grow up and become a man, but at the same time the mask indicates that you are trying to block out this vision of yourself. I see the picture of a deeply disturbed boy here, and as your mother I am very concerned."

"Don't worry so much." I wished I could explain to her that it was only a disguise. But if I told her that, I would have to explain how I planned to get into the TV, and I couldn't do that. She knew too much already. I hoped she hadn't called the cops yet.

"I think you're spending far too much time alone, Jeremy," she said. "It isn't healthy. Who did you hang out with today? A dog. What kind of friendship is that?"

I thought about telling her Solange was at this very moment lying quietly under the bed. It would prove to Mom that dogs were no trouble at all. But I decided to wait until she was in a better mood.

"Why don't you ever call up Mark or Scooter?" Mom went on. "You used to play with them a lot."

"I'm too old to play," I said.

"You know what I mean. You should give them a call."

"I will, I will," I said.

"And what are you doing in bed at six o'clock? That's unnatural. It could be a symptom of depression."

"It could just mean I have a headache," I said.

"A headache? At supper you said you had a stomach-ache. Are you sick?" She came over and felt my forehead.

"No fever. But your cheeks are flushed. They're bright pink!"

I pulled the sheet up to my eyes so she wouldn't realize it was her face powder making me pink.

"You didn't fall and hurt your head today, did you, Jeremy? Maybe you've got a concussion. That could give you a headache and stomach-ache."

"I did fall off my bike today," I said, remembering my trip home from the dump, pushing the buggy.

"I'm going to phone Dr. Suggs right away and see what he says." Mom went into her room.

I heard an ear-splitting scream. I dashed out of bed to see what had happened.

"Someone's in my bed!" she shrieked.

"Wh-wh-who?" I asked, my teeth chattering. I had a terrifying vision of Eddy Banks dressed as Goldilocks or Baby Bear resting up in Mom's room for his attack on me.

"A dog!" Mom screamed. "Out! Out, you filthy mutt! Shoo! Get out of here!"

Solange shot across the hall like a bullet, and back into my closet.

"A dog! Jeremy, how dare you get a dog when I said you couldn't!"

"It's only Solange Ricketts. I'm babysitting her while Rick's away."

"I'll talk to you about that in a minute, young man! Now get back into bed at once. You're sick."

I listened to my mom dialling, and grinned to myself. A concussion could be very convenient right now. Mom would feel too sorry for me to get mad about Solange. I put my glasses safely in a drawer, and rubbed as much of the pink powder off my cheeks as I could. Mom was gone quite a while. I heard the phone ring, and her talking. I wondered who it was. If it was the cops or the Banks Brothers I really would be sick. I got back into bed.

"Dr. Suggs said it does sound like concussion," Mom said, reappearing at my door. "Have you vomited?"

"Not yet," I said faintly, "but I feel like I might."

"He said I'm to keep a close eye on you. In fact, I have to set my alarm and wake you every hour or so during the night to make sure you haven't passed out."

"What?" There went my plans for the night.

"That was Rick who just called. I told him you were too sick to come to the phone."

"Aw, Mom!" I sat up quickly. "I've been waiting for him to call. I need to ask him some important stuff. Did you get a number?"

"No, I didn't. He said he'd call back tomorrow. One day won't make any difference."

She was wrong. One day would make *all* the difference.

"Now you lie back and get some rest," she said. "I'll be in to check you again soon. And Jeremy?"

"What?"

"I'm sorry I got mad at you. I didn't realize you were sick. You can return Rick's dog as soon as you're feeling better. And so what if you ruined your photo? It's sort of creative, in a way. You look like a cross between Zorro, Elvis, and Captain Hook." She laughed.

"It was a dumb thing to do," I admitted.

"Well, don't worry about it. Just get yourself better."

"I feel a little better already," I said. "You know, I think you're right about spending more time with friends. That's just what I'm going to do. I think I'll spend all day tomorrow with friends — maybe even overnight."

"Not so fast," she said. "We'll see how you're feeling in the morning."

"I'll be fine," I promised. "Good-night. And since I have to stay in bed — could you walk Solange for me?"

"Well, all right. But she goes home the minute you're up and walking. How can one boy get into so much mischief in one day?"

She didn't know half of what I was into. There was no hope of sneaking downstairs tonight. Not with Mom checking me every hour. But first thing tomorrow, the moment she left for work, I would put on my disguise and zap myself to the rescue. By lunchtime, if things went as planned, the aunties would be back on the couch and everything would be back to normal.

Because I'd gone to bed so early, I had no trouble waking up the next morning. I was downstairs before Mom. I was starving. All I had had to eat in the last twenty-four hours was a Jell-O sandwich and a few spoonfuls of soup. By the time she came into the kitchen I had finished a Pop-Tart, four waffles, a glass of lemonade, and three bowls of Swheatios. I was working on the fourth.

"Looks like you're back to normal," she said.

"Yes, I'm completely recovered," I said. "Personally, I don't think I had a concussion."

"You slept like a baby." She yawned. "I checked you every hour. That idiot dog barked and whined all night long. And not only that, she left a flea in my bed! I am one big itch. I got up at two and took a shower and washed my bedding. How dare you bring a fleabag mutt into this house?" She sneezed. "I think I'm allergic to her!"

I got myself another Pop-Tart.

"Are you sure you're well enough to stay here alone today, Jeremy?"

"I'm perfectly fine," I said. "If I'm not here when you get back from the theatre, don't worry. I'll just be with some of my friends."

"Who? Scooter? Mark?"

"So I'm allowed to go overnight? Thanks, Mom. You're the greatest. I'll pack my stuff right after breakfast."

"We'll see," she said. "I'm glad you're feeling better." She gave me a pat on the head. "Be good. I'll phone you at lunchtime."

The minute she was gone, I went into action. I was

wearing my green and orange zigzag shorts and a safari shirt. Over it I put on the disguise I had got ready yesterday: a black skirt of Mom's that came down to my ankles, a pair of black knee socks I found in her drawer, and my Doc Marten lace-up shoes. Deep in the ironing basket I had found a ruffled white blouse I hadn't seen Mom wear in years. It was totally wrinkled, but I ironed it, sort of. It still had wrinkles, but they were nice, straight wrinkles, not crumpled ones. Next I put on Mom's rubber swimming cap, on which I had glued about a hundred cotton balls from the bathroom. White hair made me look years older. I added a pair of white gloves, sparkly blue clip-on earrings, and a glass-bead necklace. Then I packed a big flowered purse the size of a shopping bag with supplies for the trip. I planned to be back for lunch, but you never knew. Now for the final touches. I needed to wear the radio hat on TV so I could stay in tune with what was happening in the real world. I camouflaged it with a filmy white curtain and some old Christmas bows and plastic flowers I found in the garage. Finally, I put on my reconstructed glasses and looked in the bathroom mirror. I hardly recognized myself. I had become the fourth auntie.

I stuffed a bath towel between my shirt and blouse to make myself look more womanly, and put on some pink face powder. The only problem was, I didn't look *old*. My face was the only skin showing. I wondered if soaking it in water for a long time would make it wrinkle up the way fingers and toes did. But I didn't have time for soaking. I needed something faster and more permanent. I poked around in my mom's stuff and found a bottle of beige liquid called "Porcelain Foundation." At first I thought it was something for repairing sinks, but the label said, "Apply thin layer to face and neck for smoother, younger-looking skin." I wondered if applying a thick layer would result in wrinklier, older-looking skin. I gave it a try. I found that if I put on a thick coat, or two or three, it dried and cracked like paint and made me look very old. It was the perfect finishing touch. I went downstairs, being careful not to trip on my skirt.

The big moment had finally come. My heart was thumping as I put the photo Solange had taken into the VCR slot. I sat down on the couch, holding my purse, just as the aunties must have done. I reached out — and was just about to push PLAY when the doorbell rang. I froze. Who could it be? Maybe just Mark or Scooter. But I couldn't get up and answer the door dressed like an old lady. If by chance they recognized me they would laugh their heads off. *And* I'd have to start all over and find a different disguise. This one was too good to give up. I decided to ignore the doorbell. I heard a loud knock, then a voice said, "Police! Open up!"

Chapter Fifteen

INTO THE TUBE

SOLANGE RAN TO the door, yapping excitedly.

My heart was jumping. What should I do? Rip off my costume and answer the door? Or push PLAY and zap myself out of the room before they burst in? I heard the doorknob shake.

"Police! Open up!" the voice repeated.

I pushed PLAY.

Nothing happened. Absolutely nothing.

"We're coming in," warned the voice at the door.

"Coming!" I heard myself call. "Just a minute." I ripped off my gloves, jewellery, blouse, and skirt, and kicked them under the couch. I stuffed my glasses between two couch cushions, and tossed my hat into the hall closet. I raced to the kitchen and turned on the tap. Sticking my head in the sink, I blasted cold water over my face until it was numb. I rubbed it with paper towels, and ran to open the door.

On the doorstep stood constables Rodney Heaves and Sheila Barflie.

"H-hi," I said. "C-can I help you?"

"Mind if we come in?" Constable Heaves asked.

Of course I minded, but what could I say? I hoped they would stay in the hall, but they walked right into the living room.

"We have a few questions we'd like to ask you — Jeremy, isn't it? Mind if we have a seat?"

"O-o-okay," I said faintly, jumping onto the arm of the couch and stretching my legs out so the cops wouldn't sit there and squash my glasses. I suddenly realized I was still wearing my Doc Marten shoes and black knee socks. They looked ridiculous with shorts. I hoped I had got all the makeup off my face. The constables each took an armchair.

"Is your mother home?" Constable Heaves enquired politely.

"No, I'm old enough to look after myself. I've taken the babysitting course. I can show you my certificate."

"That won't be necessary. Just relax. We just want to ask a few questions. First of all, where are your ladyfriends?"

"I'm not *that* old," I said. "My mom won't let me date. Are you kidding?"

"We *mean*," Constable Barflie said, "the three stuffed dolls that were sitting on your couch the last time we were here."

I could tell right then I was in major trouble. "Well, uh, they, uh, disappeared," I said.

"Disappeared?"

"Yes, just like that." I tried to snap my fingers, but they were still wet.

"And where are your 'dolls' now?" she asked.

"I don't exactly know," I said. "They disappeared last week — into thin air — and, uh, my mom thinks they must have been stolen or something. We really don't know what happened ..." I realized that, no matter what I said, I was in deep trouble. I only hoped they wouldn't put me in the same prison as the Banks Brothers. I didn't think I could stand that.

"I'm sure you are aware of what's been happening on TV this past week," Constable Heaves said. "In your opinion, Jeremy, would you say that the three women on TV who call themselves 'The Aunties' bear any resemblance to your three stuffed dolls?"

"I — uh — I don't — I —"

Constable Barflie got up and began prowling restlessly around the room. Solange followed, wagging her tail as if to make friends.

"We have received information to the effect that your dolls may not be what they appear to be." Constable Heaves nodded meaningfully.

"W-w-what?" I stammered, watching Constable Barflie poke around. Did the police know everything?

"We got a tip that they may not be dolls at all, but real women disguised by stocking masks."

I was so relieved I laughed out loud. "Of course my

dolls are dolls. Ask my mother. We sewed them up ourselves and stuffed them with cotton batting. What real person would have the time to sit on a couch for weeks with a stocking mask on, pretending to be a doll? Do you think I wouldn't know the difference between a doll and a dressed-up person?" I had a pretty good idea who had given them that tip.

"So you don't know anyone who likes to dress up as an elderly lady?"

"When I was downtown yesterday, I saw dozens of people dressed up as elderly ladies," I said. "Even men. There are a lot of strange people out there."

I looked for Constable Barflie. She was down on her hands and knees, near the bookshelf. Solange was sitting behind her. I thought it would be hilarious if she bit Constable Barflie in the rear.

"Could you suggest why the three women on TV were referring to someone named 'Jeremy' a day or two ago?" he asked.

I swallowed hard, and tried to think of an answer. "Um — maybe —"

"Well, I'll be doggoned!" Constable Barflie said in a nasty tone, reaching behind an armchair. "What do we have here?"

She dragged the TV I'd bought at the dump into the middle of the room. "A rewired television. Very very interesting. You're in hot water now, you little mutt." She got down on her hands and knees and peered into the back of the set.

A mutt in hot water. "Does that make me a hot-dog?" I joked, hoping to change the subject.

"Don't get smart with me, young wag, or I'll collar you so fast you'll be in the doghouse before you know what bit you!" she snarled. "Just what have you been *doing* with this television?"

"Nothing," I said.

"You can't fool a keen nose like mine! You're up to something with this TV; and I'm like a dog with a bone when it comes to a mystery."

"I bought it at the dump so I could take it apart and see what it looked like inside."

"You can't buy things from the dump!" she scoffed. "It's illegal. You won't get me off the scent that easily." She flicked on the regular TV. After a second or two of static the aunties came on. Solange started growling. I wished she would growl at the cops instead of the aunties. Whose side was she on?

"Why did the chicken cross the road?" Gladys was asking.

"I really could not hazard a guess," Mabel said.

"I know," Dotty said. "To get to the other side!"

"Ding dong, you're wrong," Gladys said. "Why did the chicken cross the road?"

"We give up," Dotty said. "Why *did* the chicken cross the road?"

"Buc-buc-buc-bucause!" Gladys cackled, and roared with laughter.

I laughed too. It was pretty funny.

Neither of the cops cracked a smile.

"Wouldn't you say," Constable Heaves said, "that those three look like real women dressed up as stuffed dolls?"

I shrugged, still giggling a little. "Kind of."

Constable Barflie was still on the floor, checking the old TV as if she thought there were wires or something connecting it to the other TV. If she looked across she would see my disguise under the couch. If she looked up a few inches she would see my picture stuck in the VCR! That was enough to make me stop laughing.

"A chicken went into the library one day," Gladys said, "and asked to borrow a book for her friend ..." Constable Heaves turned off the TV without even listening to the rest of the joke. "I think we've seen enough for today," he said. "What we've seen here is a concealed, possibly reconstructed television, and three 'missing' dolls. Or should I say women? That constitutes pretty strong circumstantial evidence, in my opinion. I think we'll be having a chat with your mother. You obviously know more than you're telling us."

"Don't talk to my mom," I said. "Please. She doesn't know anything, and anyway, she always gets things all wrong. She's a terrible witness, and she's suffering from flea bites right now so she's already upset, and if you start questioning her, I can't be responsible for what she'll do. I know you think my dolls are really dressed-up women, but they're not, honestly. And this has nothing to do with my mother."

"We'll be dogging your every move," Constable Barflie said. "We happen to know the Banks Brothers have been hounding you from prison —"

My mouth dropped open.

"Oh yes," she said. "We know more than you think. Just remember, young pup, if you lie down with dogs, you get up with fleas."

That was certainly true in my mother's case. I followed them to the door and got up enough courage to ask them, "Is it true there's a reward for getting those women off TV?"

"Yes there is," Constable Heaves said. "A big one. And there's also a big fine for withholding information from the police. So you'd only break even."

"What do you mean?" I asked.

"You're pretty smart," he replied. "Figure it out."

I thought I heard Constable Barflie growl as they went out the door.

Solange whined when they left as if she wanted to go with them. Maybe she wasn't so smart after all.

I watched from the window as they drove off, then flopped into a chair. Whew! That had been close. I was amazed they hadn't arrested me on the spot. What if they had found my disguise, or my picture in the VCR? My heart was still thumping. Did they know where Mom worked? Were they going straight to the theatre to question her? There was no phone at the theatre and I couldn't bike there faster than they could drive. What if she told them it *was* the aunties on TV? If the cops talked to her, she might come flying home to talk to *me*. With the cops *and* the Banks Brothers *and* my mom after me, the safest place for me was inside the TV. Ha, ha — even if anyone recognized me they wouldn't be able to get me out. It was the best hiding place in the world.

I had to leave a note for my mom. I thought very hard, then wrote,

Dear Mom,
You're right, I should spend more time with my friends. I'm going to see a few of them today and will probably stay overnight. Don't worry, Solange will keep you company. Back soon. I love you.
       Jeremy
       XOXOXOXOXOXOXOXOX
P.S. You'll probably see me sooner than you
    think.

Thinking about Mom made me feel a little lonely. Suppose something went wrong and I never saw her ever again. Suppose my brilliant plan for getting back out of the TV didn't work. Suppose I got stuck in there with the aunties!

A wave of panic swept over me. I decided it would be a good idea to leave word about what I was really doing — just in case ... I picked up the phone and, with a trembling finger, dialed Rick's number. But what if Rick's dad was taking Rick's messages off the machine for him while he was away? If Professor Rickett's heard my plan, he'd phone my mom right away. I'd have to risk it without an emergency backup plan. Anyway, thanks to my brilliant dream I now had a sure-fire way of getting back out of the TV. That is, if I ever figured out how to get *into* it.

Sticking my picture in the VCR slot hadn't worked. Why had it worked for the aunties and not for me? Did it have to be a metal photo, like the old tintype? Where could I get a tintype in this day and age? But — maybe, just maybe, I didn't need my own tintype. Maybe I could share the aunties'. It was worth a try. I found my mother's nail scissors and some glue. I cut around the photo of myself, being extremely careful not to trim off my ears or anything. When I was finished, I had a little paper doll of myself. I spread glue on the back and stuck it onto the aunties tintype. Now there was a fourth person in the picture: me, sprawled on the arm of the couch next to Dotty. I was sure I had finally figured out the secret of getting myself on TV. It had to work! And as for getting back out — I set the little tool suggested by my dream next to my purse on the couch, where I couldn't forget it.

I changed back into my auntie costume, wrinkles and all. I was pretty hungry by then, so I made some toast, and shared it with Solange, since she looked hungry too. I made a few extra slices and stuck them in my purse along with all my other supplies.

Solange followed me into the living room.

"Sit over there," I said. "I don't have a picture of you. You can't come with me."

I stuck the photo in the VCR, sat on the couch, reached over with the flyswatter, and pushed PLAY.

Chapter Sixteen

FAMILY REUNION

POWERFUL JOLTS LIKE enormous electrical shocks surged through my body. Deafening screeches and roars made my head pound. I felt as though I were melting, or dissolving. I felt as though every atom in my body were being disconnected and floating away. I felt as though I'd turned into liquid, or vapour, or maybe even nothing at all. All that was left of me was feelings: pain and terror. And then, after a long time, I felt a slight squeezing sensation, as if I were being squished back together again. Finally I could breathe without it hurting, and the roaring noise stopped. I felt pain in my back and neck. I opened my eyes. Mabel and Gladys were staring at me in astonishment. Next to me, Dotty had fainted away.

"Is it really you!" Gladys exclaimed.

I pulled myself up to a sitting position on the arm of the couch, and tugged the frilly blouse straight. "It's me! I made it!" I had never been so glad to see anyone in my life.

"Dear b — , dear friend, we knew you would come to help us!" Mabel said. "We are overcome with relief and gratitude."

"Wake up, Dotty, look who's here." Gladys pinched Dotty's arm. "Good news — it's J — oops, I'd better not use that name, eh? Look, it's our dear old friend, Jermima."

"What happened?" Dotty moaned. "Oh! Oh, my! You came. Oh, my dear, no face has ever looked more beautiful to me than yours." She fumbled in her purse for her fan.

"You're not exactly a knight in shining armour," Gladys said, looking with interest at my costume. "You may not be a hero, but oh, you're here!"

"That was the worst trip I've ever taken," I said. "How did you survive it?"

"It wasn't that bad," Gladys said. "A little tingly and scary, that's all."

"You call major electrical shocks tingly?" I asked.

"That is no doubt because your body contains more water than do ours," Mabel said drily. "Water conducts electricity, we understand."

"Can you tell us," Dotty asked excitedly, "is it true we're on television?"

"Yes, we are." I suddenly realized that we should be a lot more careful about what we were saying. It certainly didn't look as though we were on TV. While the aunties were exclaiming about being on the air, and giggling and poking fun at my disguise, I took a good look around. We were sitting on the same old-fashioned couch pictured in the magic tintype. Though the aunties had been in black and white in the picture and on TV, here everything was in full colour. The maroon couch was in the middle of a small, empty, cream-coloured, windowless room with a polished wooden floor. There was a wall on either side of the room, and a wall at the back. But in front of us was nothing. No cameras, no wall — nothing. I got off the couch and took a few steps forward. I seemed to bump into something. I pushed against the empty space. It was hard, like glass, but you couldn't see it, or see through it. We were staring out at complete blankness. I took a little walk around the couch, feeling the other three walls, which seemed to be normal plaster, and sat down again. Dotty and Gladys wiggled apart to make room for me between them.

"On TV!" Dotty said. "Oh, it's such a thrill." She smiled and waved at the nothingness.

"And what happens now?" asked Mabel. "I assume you have a plan."

"Yes, I have," I said. "But I've got a lot of things to tell you, and we'd better discuss them privately."

"How do you get privacy on TV?" Gladys asked. "The whole world's watching."

"Not the world," I said. "Just the province. Only a few million people." I took some red licorice out of my purse to munch on.

The only way we could get privacy was to open Gladys's flowered umbrella, put our heads close together behind it, and talk in whispers. I told the aunties all about the huge stir they had created by blocking all the other TV shows, and how people were marching in the street carrying signs, and how the radio and newspapers were full of news about them.

"But how exciting!" Dotty cried. "Fame at last. It does come to those who only sit and wait."

"So the papers are calling us Air Pirates, are they?" Gladys said. "How dashing! I always wanted to be a pirate."

"Are eyepatches in style?" Dotty asked. "I'd like one in black velvet, and a red silk bandanna for my head, and gold earrings, of course."

"I'd rather have a parrot," Gladys said. "I'd teach it to talk. *Shiver me timbers, mateys! Keelhaul your patooties! Take a flying —*"

"And did you say there were three little Mabels in the birth announcements yesterday?" Mabel interrupted, turning to me.

I nodded.

"Well, dear me. I hardly know what to say. I am, ahem, moved indeed." She raised her handkerchief to her face and made a sound as if she was blowing her nose.

I also told them about the Banks Brothers' threatening phone calls and how the robbers planned to turn me in, in exchange for their freedom. "The point is," I said, keeping my voice low, "this is all costing the TV stations millions of dollars in advertising. And the people who put the commercials on TV are furious too."

"Serves them right," Gladys said with a loud laugh. "Commercials are stupid!"

"We'll be in a truckload of trouble if we get caught," I whispered. "So you'd better be careful what you say. And don't use my name! I'm sure detectives are out there listening to every word for a clue about who we are."

"Don't worry," Gladys said. "You are now officially Aunt Jermima. Until you get us out of here, of course."

I told them how the police had come to the house, probably on a tip from the Banks Brothers.

"Those scoundrels!" Dotty cried. "Even in jail they're up to no good."

"Now that a big reward is being offered, of course they'll do anything to get it," I said. "So with the Banks Brothers after us, and the cops, and my mother doing her own investigation, I thought it might be a good idea to stay here for a day or two, at least until we figure out what to do. I brought lots of food, and told my mom I'd be spending the night with friends, so she won't be worried right away." I remembered the radio. I untied the curtain under my chin and showed them my hat.

"Brilliant, dear boy, er, friend," Mabel said, examining the batteries and and antenna. "Might I be the first to tune in? Show me how it works."

"Hey! Check out the wig, girls." Gladys pointed to the bathing cap I had covered with cotton balls. She chuckled. "Looks like somebody curled your perm too tight, Jermima.

You look like a poodle."

"Don't knock poodles," I said. "They can't help how they look. They're very intelligent dogs." The aunties exchanged hats with me while each took a turn with the radio hat.

"It's our first contact with the outside world in nearly a week," Gladys said. "Shh, it's my turn." She put on the hat. "They're talking about the protests in all major cities. Several TV stations have been vandalized. Windows smashed and workers threatened. Dear me. Shh. Wait — there's a news flash coming on. Quiet, please." She listened intently. "It's about you, D. B.," she whispered.

"Me? What is it?" I wished she'd give me the hat.

"Shh."

In a few minutes she passed the hat back. "It's just music now."

"What did they say about me?"

"They said a fourth auntie has mysteriously joined the three others on TV. 'Watchers say the new auntie, known as Jermima, seemed to appear out of nowhere. Unlike the originals, who have defied the laws of nature by not eating and barely moving in over a week, the new auntie was observed eating and walking around almost immediately. Oddly enough, this auntie, unlike the originals, appears in full colour, which media experts say bears close investigation. Are there more where this one came from? We can do nothing but wait and see.' End of broadcast," Gladys said.

"I'm probably in colour because my photo was in colour and yours wasn't," I said. "That must look weird — a black and white show with one character in colour."

"You know," Dotty said, "if we're not going back for a day or two we could do one last big show for the television audience. That would be entertaining."

"Okay," I said. "It'll help pass the time. But I'm getting hungry. I think I'll have supper first. By the way," I whispered, "five-thirty tomorrow is the deadline the Banks Brothers gave me for sending them the VCR and your reward money."

"Imagine," Mabel said. "As if they really thought anyone would be foolish enough to send it to them, just because they demanded it."

I didn't comment.

"Let them call the cops," Gladys said. "D. B. is safe here. They'll never find us. They won't be able to prove a thing."

I opened my purse and took out a can of ginger ale and a bag of Mr. Noodle. The noodles were kind of dry, but I found that if I dipped them in the ginger ale it improved the texture and flavour.

"What sort of show shall we do?" I asked. I was actually having a good time. I hadn't realized how much I'd missed the aunties. I hadn't had a minute of fun since they left my couch. Why had I ever thought they were a problem? They were three of my best friends.

"How about another exciting episode of 'Real Women/Ideal Women'?" Gladys suggested.

"No, it's been done," I said.

"Perhaps a variety show would be amusing," Dotty said. "We could all do whatever we wished."

Everyone agreed on a variety show.

It certainly didn't *feel* like we were on TV. I didn't have a bit of stage fright. There was, of course, no audience and no cameras. It wasn't much different from being alone with the aunties in my living room.

"I shall sing," Dotty said.

"I'll tell jokes," Gladys said.

"Perhaps I might give a short lecture on some topic of general interest," Mabel said. "What will you do?" she asked me.

"I'll take any one of you on in an arm-wrestling contest," I said. "I'd win, hands down. Ha, ha."

"Jermima! Really."

I kept forgetting I was an old woman. "Okay, maybe I'll dance," I said. "Since none of you can." I opened another ginger ale. I hadn't had this much fun in days.

We decided the show would start at six forty-two, just to be different.

We let Dotty open the show. She put her glove on her chest and sang five sad love songs, each with several verses. You could tell she was enjoying herself.

"What about your jokes, Gladys, dear?" Mabel said.

"What about the dog named Eileen?" I asked. "I missed it when you told it before."

"Oh," Gladys said. "What do you call a three-legged dog?"

"I don't know," I said.

"Eileen," Gladys said.

"I don't get it," I said.

She gave me a pitying look. "Oh dear, you're thick as a brick, Jermima."

"Oh, *Eileen*! I *lean*. I see," I said, catching on finally.

"I see, I see, said the blind man, and he picked up a hammer and saw!" Gladys snorted with laughter. "Say, have I ever told you my auntie jokes? What do you call an auntie who lies on the beach?"

"I don't know," I said.

"Aunt Sandy." All three aunties giggled loudly.

"Ha ha," I said.

"What do you call an auntie who takes you to court?" Gladys asked. "Auntie Sue!" She slapped her knee. "It's a good one, write it down."

"Very funny," I said.

"What do you call an auntie with a wooden leg?"

"I know," I said. "Eileen."

"Ding dong, you're wrong," Gladys said. "Aunt Peg. Ha ha! What do you call an auntie who's a whole lot smarter than you are?"

I thought very hard. Aunt Smart, Aunt Wise — no,

those didn't work.

"Give up?" she asked.

"No," I said. "Give me time." Aunt Brain, Aunt Bright —

"Time's up!" she said. "You call her Auntie Gladys! Ho ho ho! Fooled you, didn't I?"

"Hilarious," I said. "Those are dumb jokes."

"I've got a lot of uncle jokes too," she said. "They're even better. Want to hear some?"

I didn't, but she told them anyway.

"What do you call an uncle who lies on the floor?"

"What?"

"Matt! What do you call an uncle who hangs on the wall?"

"Tell me," I said. "I'm dying of curiosity."

"Art! Get it? Art! What do you call an uncle who floats in the tub? Bob!" she shouted, before I could answer. "What do you call an uncle who comes in the mail?"

I shrugged.

"Bill!" she shrieked. All three aunties were laughing so hard they could barely sit up, but I didn't think these jokes were funny at all. Especially because they were making me look ridiculous in front of a lot of people.

"What do you call —"

"Skip it," I said "on with the show."

"I think we should rename Jermima," Gladys told the others. "I think she should be named Denise."

"Why Denise?" Dotty asked.

"Because she's obviously not Denephew!" They all screeched with laughter.

I yawned. "I thought this was supposed to be a variety show," I said. "Let's have some variety. There are people out there watching, you know. If they get bored they'll turn us off."

"TV always *does* turn us off." Gladys snickered. "But okay, if you're so eager, how about that dance you promised us?"

"I'm ready," I said. I removed my hat and tuned the radio to a hot pop station. I turned up the volume good and loud and put the hat back on. Then I struck a pose and, when the next song started, I began to dance. I've never danced faster or better or longer. I boogied with my eyes closed. I snapped my fingers and shook my wig. I put one hand on the floor and danced around like that for a while. I even did a backwards somersault and waved my legs in the air. I was hot! They had great tunes on that station. I was the only one who could hear them, of course. It must have seemed a bit odd to the others watching someone dance without music. I danced till I was totally exhausted, then flopped back onto the couch.

"Yes, well," Gladys said to the invisible audience. "That was our friend, doing a peculiar dance of her own creation. If you can call it dancing. It looked more as if she had a bad case of fleas."

"We could see your knickers when you lay on the

floor like that," Mabel said. "Green and orange zigzags. Shocking."

"Your dance was certainly, ah, interesting," Dotty said kindly. "It reminds me of another song. Do you remember it, girls? 'I'm Going To Dance With the Dolly With the Hole in Her Stocking'?"

"Oh, yes," Gladys said. All three began singing loudly, taking turns adding a line: "I'm going to dance with the dolly with the hole in her stocking — and her knees keep a-knocking — and her joints keep a-squawking — and her heels keep a-rocking — and her hips keep a-locking — and her eyes keep a-gawking — and her throat keeps a-hawking — she's got black knee-high socking —"

"You're making that up as you go along," I said. "It's not funny."

"And she can't stop a-talking," Dotty sang.

"And her drawers sure are shocking," Gladys sang.

"And her friends keep on mocking," Mabel chimed in. "Our apologies, Jermima, but really, you did look rather vulgar, gyrating about like that."

"Well, on with the show," Gladys said. "Mabel, what are you planning to talk about this evening?"

"I thought I would give a brief talk on The Criminal Mind," Mabel replied.

"What would you know about the criminal mind?" I asked, still breathless from my dance, which, in spite of what they said, was pretty cool. They were just jealous.

"I have had some contact with criminals in my life, as you know," she reminded me.

"Shh," Dotty warned. "We're on TV."

"Yes," I whispered, putting Gladys's umbrella back up in front of us for privacy. "If you mean the Banks Brothers, don't give away our connection with them."

"I am not that careless," Mabel said. "I was merely going to discuss why it is that most citizens believe in the necessity of peace, order, and good government, while a certain criminal element does not."

"Sounds exciting," I said under my breath.

"However," Mabel said, "I have decided to change my topic to The Problem of Television, now that we know for certain we are on it." Mabel pushed the umbrella aside and began talking about how unhealthy television is, mentioning eye-strain, inactivity, overeating, and lack of mental exercise. Then she went on and on about how television humour isn't humour at all, but relies on artificial laugh tracks. She said advertising should be illegal, since it's immoral to encourage people to buy things they could do without. She said television gradually lowers viewers' expectations, their values, their attention span, and probably their IQ levels. I had heard it all before. I felt myself dozing off under the umbrella.

Some time later I realized that the aunties were all excited about something and were talking loudly to the audience.

"Turn us off immediately, if not sooner!" Mabel was saying. "We have a right to some privacy."

"Yes," Dotty said. "Surely you have better things to do with your time than to sit there staring. Now turn off your TVs at once, and find something useful to do."

"Yeah," Gladys added. "Quit spying on us. Peeping Toms!"

I glanced at my watch. It was nine a.m. I had slept a full twelve hours! The umbrella had fallen to the floor. My head was cushioned in Gladys's big soft lap. The rest of my body was so stiff it hurt to move. And my earrings were killing me.

"What's going on?" I asked.

"Mabel has just made an excellent twelve-hour argument in favour of people on TV having a right to privacy," Dotty explained. "It's not fair that anyone who wishes can turn on a television and spy on us at any time of the day or night. We have no privacy whatsoever!"

Her words made me think of something that put all other thoughts out of my head.

"Uh — forget what I said about staying here for a couple of days," I said. "We've got to go back — right away!"

Chapter Seventeen

THE MAGIC WORD

"WHAT'S THE BIG hurry?" Gladys asked, as I stood up. "I thought you wanted to stay awhile. Get your two cents' worth on TV while you had a chance."

"That was yesterday," I said. "I've changed my mind. Stay if you want to, but I'm leaving. Right now."

"He misses his dear mother," Dotty said.

"That's not it," I said. "Come on, let's go. I'll explain later." I crossed my legs tightly.

"Why have you got your face twisted up like that?" Gladys asked. "And why are you hopping around with your legs crossed? Is it some new kind of dance?"

Mabel murmured something I couldn't hear. Dotty put her glove to her mouth.

"Oho! Is that it?" Gladys asked. "You mean you have to go to the bathroom?"

I felt my face get hot. I crossed my legs tighter, and nodded. Why hadn't I thought of this problem before?

"Do a dance, take a chance, wet your pants — don't wet your aunts!" Gladys chuckled.

"We can be ready in a few minutes," Mabel said. "Get your things together, girls."

I sat back on the couch behind the umbrella. This was not a situation I wanted to discuss in front of millions of viewers. "I hope I can wait that long," I said.

"When you gotta go, you gotta go, and if you don't go when you gotta go, you find out you've already gone!" Gladys said. "How dry I am," she sang, "how wet I'll be, if old D. B. wee-wees on me."

"Gladys!" Mabel said sharply. "Where did you learn such disgraceful rhymes?"

"So how *are* you going to get us home, dear?" Dotty asked. "We racked our brains and couldn't figure out how to get back. You are so clever to have thought of a plan. What is it?"

I pulled the remote control out of my purse and waved it around triumphantly. "Ta-da!"

Gladys raised her eyebrows. "We're obviously *remote* from where we want to be, and the situation has got out of *control*, but what's your point?"

"Well," I explained, "when you three zapped yourselves in here, you punched the VCR buttons rather than the remote control buttons, right?"

"That's right," Gladys said. "I reached across with the flyswatter and pressed PLAY on the VCR machine. After all, we didn't want your remote control zapped along with us."

"But the remote control is the key to getting back!" I said. "At least, it better get us back."

I quickly told them about Earl at the dump, and my dream of being trapped in a garbage compactor while he kept turning his uniform inside-out and urging me to buy a remote control. "So you see," I said, "that's when I figured that I'd have to get you out of the TV from the *inside out*. Pressing the buttons from the living room didn't have any effect. I decided I'd have to join you in here and zap the remote control from this end."

"How brilliant of you," Dotty cried. "We're ready to go. Goodbye!" She waved. "Oh, goodbye, all you lovely people out there in TV land. It's been delightful. A pleasure."

"Eenie meenie minie moe," Gladys said. "Press the button and off we go!"

I pointed the remote control in front of me and pressed EJECT. Nothing happened. I tried again. And again. I quickly pressed REWIND and FAST FORWARD, and every other button on the converter. Nothing happened. "I — I thought it would work —" I began. I shook it, and pressed the buttons harder. "I can't believe it didn't —" I was afraid to look at the aunties. "I — I guess the remote control *doesn't* work from in here. I guess I was wrong. I'm sorry — I — What are we going to do?"

"I can't believe it," Gladys said. "You came here to rescue us without really knowing how to get back? "

"I *had* a plan," I protested. "Can I help it that it didn't work? Do you have a better one?"

"Your inside-out idea was no more than a dream." Mabel sighed deeply.

"Don't blame me," I said. "I tried." I was thinking of the many terrible consequences of being a human being trapped on TV. The first one was that I was going to be very embarrassed if I didn't get to a washroom fast.

"Blame you?" Dotty cried. "On the contrary. To think that you came all this way, not being certain you'd get back, just for us! It's an act of courage and loyalty such as I have never seen before! You are a brave and selfless friend."

"It was a daring act," Gladys said. "A leap of faith into the vast unknown."

"There are not many who would do what you have just done," Mabel said. "Your devotion is truly beyond compare."

"Well, I wouldn't have done it for just anyone," I told them. "I realized when you were gone how much I missed you — and besides, I had to get you out or I'd be in trouble with the law."

"Missed us?" Mabel asked. "You truly missed us, dear boy?"

"Does this mean you want us in your life after all?" Dotty cried. "You weren't hoping to get rid of us?"

"You mean you actually *like* us?" Gladys asked.

"Of course I like you," I said. "I thought you knew that. I was lonely when you were gone. Life seemed kind of empty without you there on the couch." My face felt warm. I felt happy and silly and embarrassed all at the same time.

"He loves us!" Dotty cried. "Oh, girls, have any words ever sounded sweeter to your ears?"

"Well, well," Mabel said, "in that case, we need not have gone to all that trouble to make up our farewell poem. If you are truly fond of us, perhaps we shall consider staying. But the first order of business is still to get out of here — back to the couch. We shall all have to put on our thinking caps."

"I hope you don't mean that awful leather helmet," Gladys said. "It's too tight. They were a waste of money."

"Don't complain, dear," Dotty said. "Think."

We all sat there thinking about how to get back to my living room. I ate some peanuts and some more licorice twizzlers from my purse. Gladys gave me a jawbreaker from hers. I thought as hard as I could. There had to be a way out of here. There just had to be. And we had to find it in a hurry. I crossed my legs again

"We'll never get home," I whispered. "It's hopeless."

"Nonsense," Mabel said. "One must *never* give up hope. Where there is a will there is always a way."

We thought for a very long time. Gladys kept twirling the umbrella in an annoying way. I felt uncomfortably warm. It seemed as though the little room we were in had got smaller and hotter. I needed air. How much air was left? The three aunties could stay there indefinitely. They didn't need air or food or water or a bathroom. But I could die if I didn't get out of there soon. I had never imagined myself dying in front of an audience of millions. Either I would die of a burst bladder, or millions of TV viewers would watch me grow weaker and thirstier by the hour, until I went crazy from thirst. My mouth felt like chalk. A flake of porcelain makeup fell off my face and landed in my lap. It had begun already. I was drying up and fading away. I wondered if Mom would be watching when I drew my last breath. My life began to pass before my eyes. It wasn't the greatest life. If I ever get out of here alive, I thought, I promise to be a better kid. I'll obey my mom and always do what she asks me to — even clean the garage. I'll be nicer to the aunties. I'll be thoughtful and generous and kind. I won't be greedy. I won't be envious of Rick and all his stuff. "If we get back alive I'll be a totally different kid — no one will even recognize me."

"Especially in this get-up you're wearing." Gladys laughed loudly.

I hadn't realized I'd spoken aloud.

"We pressed PLAY to get here," Mabel said to the others. "Perhaps ... if someone out there pressed FAST FORWARD on the VCR it would get us back to D. B.'s living room."

"What about REWIND?" Gladys asked. "Wouldn't it be more likely to get us there?"

"You're both wrong," I said. "I pressed REWIND *and*

FAST FORWARD and neither did anything except make you smaller or larger on the screen."

"Which made us larger?" Mabel asked.

"FAST FORWARD," I said.

"How large did it make us?" she asked in an excited whisper.

"You got bigger and bigger until all I could see was Gladys's big fat nose getting so huge I was afraid it would burst through the screen any minute, so I quick pressed REWIND and got you back to normal size and —"

"Burst through the screen," Mabel repeated. "Do you realize what you just said, dear boy? Another few seconds of fast forward and I do believe we *would* have burst through the screen. We would have been back in your living room."

"You mean I could have got you back that easily?" I gasped. "You mean — ?"

"She means you blew it," Gladys said. "Thanks a whole lot!"

"Anyway," Dotty said sadly, "now that D. B. is here with us, there's no one left to press the VCR buttons."

"Did you bring anything with you that might help?" Gladys asked. "Like a hammer or pickaxe? You could bash down the walls. Maybe we could escape that way. What's in your purse?"

"Food." I opened it up. I still had five bags of Mr. Noodle, a chocolate bar, two slices of toast, and three cans of ginger ale."

"What good is food to us?" Gladys sighed.

"Well, if it makes you feel any better, the food doesn't do me much good either," I said. "Toast and noodles and chocolate will only make me thirsty, then I'll have to drink the pop, and that will make me have to go to the bathroom even worse — it's a vicious circle!"

I was starving, too. Six licorice twizzlers, some peanuts, and a jawbreaker were not exactly what I called breakfast. I opened my purse and reached for a slice of — "Toast!" I shouted. "I've got toast!"

"Hush, D. B., keep your voice down, I beg you," Mabel said.

"He's gone mad," Gladys murmured.

"No," I whispered excitedly, waving the toast in front of them. "Solange, Rick's poodle, is at my place. She's very smart. If she can push a button on the Polaroid camera, I bet she can push a button on the VCR too!" I shoved aside the umbrella and jumped off the couch. The aunties began to protest, but I ran right up to the nothingness in front of us and waved the toast invitingly. I gave a little whistle, and made kissing noises the way Rick does to call her. "Want some toast?" I asked. "Come on, girl, want some toast? It's all yours. Just push that little FAST FORWARD button and you've got it. Come on."

"Stop, oh, D. B., do wait a moment," Dotty whispered.

"Get back here, you imbecile," Gladys hissed.

"Please," Mabel added, "come back to the couch at

once."

I turned to face them.

"Please," Mabel said sternly, "you must come back behind the umbrella so we can discuss this."

I squeezed onto the couch again. All three of them looked upset. "What's the big deal?" I asked. "I finally get a plan and now you try to stop me."

"Your plan has a number of flaws," Mabel said. "First of all, if your mother is at work, I doubt very much that your television at home is turned on. Therefore, this clever poodle will not be able to see you capering about with the toast. Secondly, even if your television is on and the dog can see you, how do you know which button, if any, she will push? She might push EJECT and pop our picture right out of the VCR. Thirdly, and most importantly, even if the dog managed to push the correct button to transport us safely home, *you*, my dear boy, were not sitting on the couch with us. You would very likely have been left behind as the three of us were whisked back to your living room. Where would you be then?"

"Oh," I said, in a small voice. "I guess you're right." It was hopeless. There was no way out. I put my head in my hands, too discouraged to think any more.

"Oh — oh my! I feel — I do believe I feel a tingling sensation," Dotty said.

I was thrown back against the couch cushions as though I'd been hit by a bolt of electricity.

"Hold onto your hats," Gladys shouted. "We're going somewhere!"

I felt a familiar surge of pain through my body as my atoms began to disconnect. It's very frightening to feel yourself rapidly decomposing. I felt jolted and squashed, expanded and contracted. A roaring sound filled my ears. The experience was at least as noisy and painful as the first time. This time, though, I felt a little safer. I had survived it before. And this time I wasn't alone. Wherever we ended up, at least I'd be with the aunties. After what seemed like a long time, I finally felt myself being squeezed back together. I heard a high-pitched whine, and landed with a soft thud. I opened my eyes. We were back! Back on the couch in my living room! The whining was coming from Solange, who had been lying on the couch when we arrived, and was frantically trying to burrow out from beneath Gladys's large bottom.

"We're home!" I shouted. "We made it! Whew! Am I glad *that's* over."

"So you're back," said a voice from the armchair.

Chapter Eighteen

PIRATES' REWARD

I LOOKED UP in terror.

Rick was sitting across from me, grinning.

"What are *you* doing here?" I asked.

"I told you I was getting back on Thursday. It's Thursday. I came looking for Solange. And you, of course."

As the aunties rearranged their skirts and hair, I briefly told Rick what had happened since he'd left.

"Wow!" he said. "Compared to your adventures, Calgary was pretty quiet. It was TV as usual out there." He told us how he had arrived at my place only about five minutes ago, and turned on the TV to see me dressed as an auntie, waving a piece of toast around. "I thought you'd gone nuts! Solange went nuts too. She ran up to the TV and jumped and yapped like crazy. She started pushing every button she could find, with her nose. I didn't know what was going on. You had said something about FAST FORWARD, so I pushed it, and suddenly you were off the TV and here on the couch!"

I turned to look at the TV. The screen was filled with grey staticky snow.

"Our photo is still in the VCR slot," Mabel pointed out.

I carefully pressed EJECT. Out popped our picture. A commercial for toilet-bowl cleaner appeared on the screen. It was the kind guaranteed to make your toilet bowl as sparkling clean as the bowls you eat out of.

"That reminds me," I said, and raced to the bathroom. Ah, the comfort of a bathroom! While I was there I took off my costume and washed the crusty makeup off my face. I also found my glasses frames and stuck my lenses back into them. It took me a while.

When I got back to the living room, I heard a strange roar coming from outside.

"What's that noise?" I asked.

"It sounds like millions of people cheering," Gladys said. "I guess they're happy their TVs are working again."

"Oh, I missed this room," Dotty said. "I truly did. Oh, Jeremy — now we can call you Jeremy again — oh, Jeremy, it was so dreadfully good of you to come after us and rescue us."

"So tell me everything that happened," Rick said, as Solange licked his face and arms. The aunties and I told him the whole story, from start to finish — including the part about Solange's amazing photographic abilities.

"So the aunties figured out a way to get on TV," Rick said, "but then couldn't figure out how to get off it."

"That's where Jeremy came in," Dotty said. "Jeremy to the rescue. He came all the way in there — so brave — and saved us."

"We were just lucky," I said looking at the floor. I had put my faith in a remote control. But I had never been even remotely in control.

"Do you realize," Rick said excitedly, "that if this worked once it could work again? You could get on TV any time you wanted. Whenever you were bored, or wanted to replace some dumb show, you could just zap your photo back in there!"

"Not me," I said. "It hurt. I felt like an ant being squeezed through an accordion by a steroid-crazed bench-presser. Besides, I'd have to get back into my dumb disguise again. And anyway, I think everybody's too suspicious of us now. We got away with it this time. If we tried it again, they'd nail us. Even now, the cops know I'm involved. They could come knocking on the door any minute."

"That is very true," Mabel said. "That is why we must protect you. You rescued us. Now it is our turn to help you. Pass me the telephone, if you please. I wish to place a call."

"Yes, make yourselves scarce for ten minutes," Gladys said. "The three of us have a few things to do. We need to get those cops off our case permanently. We discussed this problem while you were sleeping last night, Jeremy, and came up with a plan."

"What? What are you up to?" I asked. "Who are you calling?"

"Just trust us, and do as you're told," Gladys said.

"We want to surprise you," Dotty added.

"I don't want any more surprises," I said.

"Come on," Rick said. "Solange needs a little walk anyway."

I went out with Rick and Solange, wondering what was going on. How could the aunties stop the police from suspecting me? They would only cause more trouble.

"Wait here," I said to Rick in the driveway. "I'll be right back." I went inside and sneaked up the stairs. I slipped into my mother's bedroom and picked up the extension phone just in time to hear Mabel say, "This is legal council for Mr. Edward Banks. Can you please put him on the line?"

I stifled a gasp. What was she doing calling the Banks Brothers? Was she *trying* to get me arrested? In a few minutes I heard Eddy Banks's rough voice say, "Yeah? Who is this? Whaddaya want?"

"My name is Mabel Dermott," Mabel said, "and I am speaking on behalf of my young friend Jeremy, and my sister Gladys, and my cousin Dotty.

"You — you mean you're one of them aunties, off the TV?"

"That is correct," Mabel said. "I am now off the television, and I require your prompt co-operation in an important matter."

"Why should we co-operate with yous?" Eddy asked. "What's in it for us?"

I was wondering the same thing.

"I propose to you that you and your brothers accept the blame for the fact that there have been no programs on television all week," Mabel said calmly.

"What?" Eddy said, and laughed. "Who do you think you're messing with, lady? Why would we do a dumb thing like that, huh?"

"I trust you will hear me out like a gentleman," Mabel said, "and then I think you will agree to my plan."

"Not ruddy likely," Eddy said. "Maybe I'll hang up, instead."

"Excuse me a moment," Mabel said. "Jeremy, are you by any chance eavesdropping on the upstairs telephone? If so, please hang up immediately. Thank you very much."

I hung up, embarrassed, and came back downstairs. Mabel was still talking to Eddy.

"Go walk that nasty little — I mean that *clever* little dog," Gladys said.

"But be back in ten minutes," Dotty added. "Time is of the essence."

I joined Rick outside and we walked Solange around the block a couple of times. I told him what the aunties were up to.

"It'll never work, whatever it is," Rick said. "Why should the Banks Brothers co-operate with the aunties? They'll never agree to take the blame for messing up the TV all week. They're not that stupid."

I agreed. "The aunties are good at talking people into things," I said. "But not that good."

Mabel, Gladys, and Dotty were waiting impatiently when we got back inside.

"Quickly, Jeremy, help us out of our clothing," Mabel said.

"What? Me? Take your clothes off? Are you out of your minds?"

"Believe us, it's necessary," Gladys said. "Desperate circumstances require desperate measures. The courier's going to be here in a few minutes."

"I can't undress you!" I said. "What are you talking about?"

"We can't wait for your mother to do it," Dotty said. "There can be no false modesty. Quickly, undo our buttons, and pull our dresses over our heads for us. We cannot do it alone. There are extra clothes in the box beneath the couch. Hurry, please."

"Not until you tell me what this is all about," I said.

"It's about saving your skin, that's what," Gladys said. "Now get a move on. It's almost noon. If we're going to make the six o'clock news, we've got to scramble. Our clothes are going to be couriered to Kingston, and even with a speed demon of a courier, that takes a few hours."

"You mean you want the Banks Brothers to dress up in these clothes and pretend *they* were the air pirates? You're crazy! They'll never do it."

"Trust us," Mabel said.

"The cops will trace the courier back to us so fast it won't be funny," Rick said. "We'll end up in way more trouble than we're in now."

"It's not that kind of courier," Gladys said. "It's Jake 'Speed' Spencer, one of Eddy Banks's pals on the outside."

"You mean you're getting us mixed up with more criminals? You're kidding!"

"Patience," Mabel said. "Do trust us. Have we ever let you down before?"

I sighed. Yes, they had. But they were hard to argue with, and they outnumbered Rick and me. Reluctantly we helped them change into different dresses. We packed their TV outfits in a bag, and when the doorbell rang we passed it to Speed Spencer, a thin, shifty-eyed man who grabbed the package and was gone before we got a good look at him.

"Now get some money out of the couch cushions so we can reimburse your dear mother for our call to Kingston," Mabel said. "Then we shall wait for the evening news."

The three of them refused to say one more word about what they were up to. They seemed quite calm and pleased with themselves. It drove me crazy. Any minute I expected the cops to burst in and arrest us. While we waited, the aunties read up on themselves in the newspapers.

"Our names in print," Dotty breathed. "Oh my, we're famous! Celebrities!"

"More like fugitives from justice," Gladys said. "It's a dream come true!"

"I find all this publicity a trifle vulgar," Mabel said. But she read the articles as eagerly as the others.

"Say," Dotty said. "Listen to this ad in the personals: 'Financially secure, young-at-heart gentleman wishes to meet three charming ladies of "The Aunties Show" fame. Enjoys conversation, fine wines, and adventure. Drives gold Cadillac. Anxiously awaiting your reply to Box 249. Bob.' Do you think we should write to him, girls? He sounds rather fun."

The aunties giggled.

The time passed slowly. I spent it trying to figure out how I would explain things to my mom when she got home. I tried to get the aunties and Rick to help me, but they were too busy reading, and laughing.

When Mom arrived, just before six, I gave her a big hug. "Am I glad to see you!" I said. "I missed you!"

"What's this all about?" she asked. "You were only gone overnight. But next time tell me *where* you're going, okay? I wasn't sure if you were at Mark's or Scooter's. I didn't get an answer at Mark's, and Scooter's number is unlisted. I was a little concerned." She gave me a hug back. "I missed you too. Don't run off on me like that again."

"I promise I won't," I said. "And I promise to clean up the garage, first thing tomorrow." I was making a start on my promise of becoming a better kid.

"It's about time," she said. "I found an old baby buggy out there that I've never seen before in my life. I think the neighbours are starting to throw their junk in our garage too. This place is getting out of control. Did you know" — she lowered her voice — "it's been such a long time since I've done any cleaning around here that yesterday I looked behind a chair and found an old, broken TV I don't even remember? It's shocking. It must have been there for years!"

She suddenly gave me a very strange look. I wondered if I had said something that made her suspicious. But she was staring at my neck. I put my hand up and felt the glass bead necklace.

She looked lower. "Are black knee socks with shorts in style?" she asked. "And are bead necklaces for boys the latest fad? I know kids have their own taste in clothes, but really, Jeremy, you look very weird."

"I, uh, thought I looked cool," I stammered. "Did you watch TV last night?" I wanted to know if she had seen me in my Jermima disguise.

"No, did you? Someone told me there was a fourth auntie on. The audacity! How dare those thieves copy our idea? We should have got a patent. I heard they made this one walk, and dance, and appear to eat and drink. It must have been done with strings, or robotics. Was their auntie better than ours?"

"Definitely better looking," I said. I heard a growl

from Gladys in the living room. "Uh — that must be Solange," I said.

"We have to talk about that dog," Mom said. "Last night she chewed up my pink slippers. This morning when I let her out she dug a hole in the flower bed. Then Rick's dad phoned to say you had forgotten her appointments at the vet's and the beauty parlour, and *I* ended up having to rebook them. She's got to go!" She walked towards the living room.

"Uh — Rick's back," I said.

"So I see," my mother said. "And I see the TV is mysteriously working again!" Rick was sitting in an armchair, reading a newspaper and watching TV, and listening to Mom's radio hat all at the same time. "I see you decided to bring the aunties back," Mom said coldly. "As well as my hat!" She snatched it off his head. "Maybe you'd like to explain just what you've been up to, Rick."

Rick looked blank. "Huh?" he asked. "What do you mean?"

"You know very well what I mean," she said. "Now I want an explanation of exactly what you've been doing this week. And don't try to spin me some story. I want the truth."

"I — I was in Calgary," Rick said in a confused way. "I — I didn't take your hat or —"

"Richard Ricketts!" Mom warned. "Tell the truth, or I will — I *knew* Rick was behind this!" she said to me. "I knew it! All the clues pointed to him. He had access to our house and the aunties. I bet you brought the aunties back in that baby carriage parked in the garage. I bet you never were in Calgary, were you?"

Rick still looked completely confused.

"You did it with videos, didn't you!" Mom went on. "It's amazing to me that a young boy, with little more than a basic computer and video machine, was actually able to wipe entire stations off the air for a week! I don't know whether to be angry or impressed. I suppose," she added, "this means we won't be collecting the reward. All my hard investigative work for nothing —"

"Shh," I interrupted. "The news is coming on!"

"I have a good mind to report you to the police, Rick." Mom said. "Whether I get a reward or not. Theft is theft."

"Sit down, Mom," I said. "Please. We really want to watch the news and see the — uh — find out what's been happening. Don't you?" I had my fingers crossed that the aunties' plan would work. I wished I believed in their plan as much as they had believed in mine.

"In fact," Mom said, "I believe I *will* report you. Right after my theatre meeting. I just have time to change and grab a snack and get there on time."

The six o'clock news came on, with the usual C-KIT music, and the announcement: "All the news you need from the people you trust!"

"You mean there's some news we don't need? From people we shouldn't trust?" I asked.

My mother didn't even smile. While the announcer commented about finally being back on the air, she kept talking, getting more and more upset with Rick. "Thought you could exchange our aunties for your little dog, did you?" she asked him. "Well, you won't get away with it. No, you've stolen our dolls, my radio hat, and several television stations. You're a negative influence on Jeremy, and I am going to have to ask you to leave and never come back again. I can't have you teaching Jeremy such sneaky and illegal behaviour. Does your father have any idea of the things you've been up to while he's at work? Calgary, huh! I think you'd better grab your little dog and scram, before I get really upset."

Fortunately, the announcer said, "We now bring you this late-breaking news regarding the three air pirates who effectively cancelled television shows across the province until today. The mystery has finally been solved. The three aunties have identified themselves as Edward, Mortimer, and Harvey Banks, three prisoners at the Kingston Penitentiary. Our on-the-scene reporter brings you the details."

My mother gasped. "What! Shh! Listen!"

The three Banks Brothers appeared on the screen, wearing stocking masks and dressed in the clothes that had been on the aunties just a few hours before. Mort wore Mabel's navy-blue suit and small black hat. Harv, in the middle, was wearing Gladys's pink and grey flowered dress, necklaces, and holey stockings. Eddy had squeezed himself into Dotty's green and white dress and straw hat covered with flowers. They had got wigs from somewhere, and makeup, and they wore gloves and held the aunties' purses. They admitted with proud smirks that they were the air pirates.

"Police spokespersons refused to comment on whether the swaggering inmates actually went so far as to boldly taunt them with trumped-up tips on innocent citizens, as the brothers claim. It is not known at this point just how the Banks Brothers managed to pull off their remarkable act of piracy. They also refuse to identify the mysterious fourth auntie, hinting that she was one of their many friends 'on the outside.' More on the story later. Now, back to our regular newscast."

I saw Gladys nudge Mabel and Dotty.

"Oh, Rick," Mom said. "Oh — I owe you an apology. Oh — I misjudged you. Here I am, jumping to conclusions, accusing an innocent boy, when all the time professional criminals were responsible. Those Banks Brothers! I suppose they got the idea from seeing our aunties when they broke in here and you captured them. But I still don't understand — if the Banks Brothers were the women on TV, where did our aunties disappear to?"

"Uh — they never — uh — actually left this room," I said. "I — uh — just misplaced them for awhile, but then I found them again, and —"

"Just like I found that old TV behind the armchair," Mom said, nodding. "Really, Jeremy, we've *got* to get a grip on housecleaning around here before we lose each other. I'll make out a schedule for dusting and scrubbing first thing tomorrow."

"Can Rick stay for supper?" I asked.

"Certainly," Mom said. "Of course. Although there isn't much to eat in the house. I'll leave you a bit of money and you can order a pizza. I hate to run out on you, but my theatre meeting has been rescheduled for tonight. I won't be late. Be good now, you two, and stay out of mischief. I apologize again for suspecting you, Rick." She went upstairs to change.

❖

After Mom left, Rick and I ordered our favourite pizza, a deep-dish double-cheese Hawaiian ham and pineapple deluxe specialissimo with olives.

"So now the Banks Brothers are saying I'm their friend!" I said.

"We looked much better on TV than they did, of course," Dotty said, "but they weren't bad."

"How did you ever get the Banks Brothers to say they were air pirates?" Rick asked Mabel. "I can't believe it! Aren't they letting themselves in for a lot of trouble? What did you tell them?"

"We simply told them it was their fault we got on the air in the first place," Mabel said. "After all, you bought the VCR that caused the problem with money you got from *their* capture. So they must share the blame as our accomplices. Unfortunately, they did not fall for that, so I had to use a more convincing argument."

"She asked them if they valued TV," Gladys went on. "Of course they do. There isn't much else to do in prison. Mabel reminded them that if they turned us in to the police, we would have to hide. And of course the safest hiding place is back on TV. And next time, she told them, we might *never* come out. That would mean no TV ever again! They didn't like that idea."

"But what about the reward?" I asked. "The one offered for getting them off the air. No questions asked. Are criminals allowed to get rewards for doing illegal things?"

"No," Dotty said. "Of course they can't claim the reward. And since they're in prison already, it's unlikely they'll be prosecuted. They've already got long sentences. And no money to pay fines. *But* — they may be able to collect the other reward."

"What other reward?" Rick asked.

"The PQE reward," Gladys said. "It was in yesterday's paper. Parents for Quality Entertainment have offered a reward to whoever got the aunties *on* the air. The Banks Brothers will get that, and they'll be able to sell their 'story' to the magazines as well!"

"They know that if they ever turn us in," Mabel went on, "if the police ever suspect us, and we disappear into the TV again, they will be considered accomplices, *and* exposed as fraudulent aunties, *and* they will probably have to give back the PQE reward. It is much simpler if they simply take credit for being the original air aunties."

"But won't the other prisoners make mincemeat of them?" I asked.

"That is what they were afraid of," Mabel said. "I instructed them on the virtues of sharing. The PQE reward is much smaller than the other reward would have been, but it is still enough to share. Perhaps it is enough to buy each prisoner his own TV. The Banks Brothers may become prison heroes. Besides, the mystery of their accomplishment is bound to impress their fellow inmates."

"I hope we've heard the last of them," Dotty said. "They should get a life."

"They should get a life sentence," Gladys said.

Rick turned to the aunties. "But the three of you are always saying you can't stand TV. So why did you want to be on it?"

The aunties looked at each other. "What, pray tell, do you think the point of our little escapade was?" Mabel asked.

"You wanted to be on television so you could criticize it and boycott it?" Rick asked.

"Ding dong," Gladys said. "We never planned to go on TV at all. It was an accident."

"We did not plan to get stuck in the television," Mabel said. "Our well-laid plan, you might say, went awry."

"Yes, if you had read the note we left Jeremy, you'd

understand," Dotty said.

The pizza arrived just then. I set it on the coffee table while I fetched the aunties' farewell poem.

Rick read it, looking puzzled.

"With careful thought and planning we've decided
(It's best for you and us, we strongly feel)
To leave the stuffy modern world of dollhood
And go back to the days when we were real.

"We've had some laughs, dear boy, we'll truly miss you,
We hope you know it's been a hard decision.
And if we could, we'd surely take you with us
In to the past — by way of television.

"You mean you thought you could go back to your past by sticking your photo into the VCR? Go back to the time when you were real?" Rick laughed.

"Yes," Gladys said. "That's exactly what we were trying to do. So now you know."

"They thought the TV would work sort of like a time machine," I explained to Rick. "Some time machine. More like a time bomb."

"On the contrary," Mabel said. "I believe it worked rather well."

"What do you mean?" I asked. "It didn't take you back to your own time."

"Perhaps not," Mabel agreed, "but PLAY got us on TV, and FAST FORWARD brought us back here ..."

"Which should tell you something, Jeremy," Gladys added. "Are you thinking?"

"You mean you actually think REWIND would have taken you back into your time?"

"Bingo!" Gladys said. "Worth a try, don't you think?"

"You mean you plan on going back again? Back to the past? Without me?"

"Unless, of course, you would like to come with us." Dotty smiled.

"Me? Back into the past? With the three of you? I — I don't know," I said, slowly.

"Not immediately, of course," Mabel said. "A trip that includes you would require very careful planning. Next time, we will do it right."

"Do you think it's possible?" I asked. "We could really go back to your time?"

"Why not?" Gladys asked.

"Wow!" I said. "It's — amazing!"

"It's our best plan yet," Dotty said proudly.

"You may not have got the reward," Rick told me. "But which is better: the reward, or your very own personal time machine?"

I was so amazed by the possibilities ahead of us that I was speechless.

"I hate to tell you," Gladys said, "but while we've been

talking, that four-legged little beast has been gobbling up your supper."

I looked at the coffee table. Solange was licking crumbs from the empty pizza box.

"I'll put her in the backyard before she gets sick on the carpet," Rick said.

"Who needs a dog?" I said to the aunties when Rick left the room. "They're too much trouble, and they can't think, you know, or have good ideas or dream up brilliant plans and adventures."

When Rick came back in Mabel said, "Gladys and Dotty and I would be pleased to treat you to another of those deep-ham cheesy deluxe double apple Hawaiianissimo special pine olive pizza dishes, since your first one is now in the backyard. Our reward money is still in the couch cushions. Let us party, as they say!"

"Yes, let's!" Dotty cried happily, getting out the Snap cards.

"Party down!" Gladys bellowed.

"Right on!" Rick said. "We've got a lot to celebrate."
I smiled. "That's true. Great friends, wild adventures, and an exciting — a timeless — future!"

❖

Also in the series:
JEREMY AND THE AUNTIES

FELICITY FINN *writes adult novels and plays
as well as books for young people. She and
her family live in rural Ontario.*